THE HOTTEST DADDY

A SINGLE DADDY ROMANCE COLLECTION

MICHELLE LOVE

HOT AND STEAMY ROMANCE

CONTENTS

About the Author	vii
Sign Up to Receive Free Books	ix
Blurb	xi
Prologue	1
1. Chapter One	5
2. Chapter Two	10
3. Chapter Three	22
4. Chapter Four	28
5. Chapter Five	36
6. Chapter Six	45
7. Chapter Seven	51
8. Chapter Eight	60
9. Chapter Nine	70
10. Chapter Ten	79
11. Chapter Eleven	82
12. Chapter Twelve	86
13. Chapter Thirteen	91
14. Chapter Fourteen	97
15. Chapter Fifteen	102
16. Chapter Sixteen	109
17. Chapter Seventeen	114
18. Chapter Eighteen	120
19. Chapter Nineteen	128
20. Chapter Twenty	136
21. Chapter Twenty-One	142
22. Chapter Twenty-Two	147
23. Chapter Twenty-Three	153
Sign Up to Receive Free Books	157
Preview of The Virgin's Dance	158
Chapter One	161
Chapter Two	166
Chapter Three	173

Chapter Four	177
Chapter Five	185
Chapter Six	189
Chapter Seven	194
Chapter Eight	200
Other Books By This Author	209
About the Author	211
Copyright	213

Made in "The United States" by:

Michelle Love

© Copyright 2020 – Michelle Love

ISBN: 978-1-64808-141-5

ALL RIGHTS RESERVED. No part of this publication may be reproduced or transmitted in any form whatsoever, electronic, or mechanical, including photocopying, recording, or by any informational storage or retrieval system without express written, dated and signed permission from the author

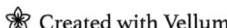 Created with Vellum

ABOUT THE AUTHOR

Mrs. Love writes about smart, sexy women and the hot alpha billionaires who love them. She has found her own happily ever after with her dream husband and adorable 6 and 2 year old kids.

Currently, Michelle is hard at work on the next book in the series, and trying to stay off the Internet.

"Thank you for supporting an indie author. Anything you can do, whether it be writing a review, or even simply telling a fellow reader that you enjoyed this. Thanks

facebook.com/HotAndSteamyRomance
instagram.com/michellesromance

SIGN UP TO RECEIVE FREE BOOKS

Sign Up to Receive Free E-Books and Audiobook Codes.

Would you like to read **The Unexpected Nanny, Dirty Little Virgin** and **other romance books** for **free**?

You can sign up to receive these free e-books and audiobooks by typing this link into your browser:

https://www.steamyromance.info/free-books-and-audiobooks-hot-and-steamy/

Or this one:

https://www.steamyromance.info/the-unexpected-nanny-free/

BLURB

Sunday

I left everything behind to save my own life. Everything.
What I didn't count on was finding him… River Giotto, the handsomest, sexiest man I've ever met.
My body has no control when he's near, I crave his touch, his lips on mine, his skin on my skin…
His cock buried deep inside me.
I might have lost my identity, but I found the love of my life…
I just hope no-one takes him away from me.
Or me away from him.

River

Just when my life was falling apart, Sunday came into it.
God, I can't stop thinking about her, her face, her hair, her beautiful, curvy body…

The way she gasps my name when she comes...
She is my life now, my whole life, and nothing and no-one will stop us from being together...
Nothing...

PROLOGUE

February, one year ago ...

HE CLOSED his eyes and listened to her voice, the way he always did when the camera moved from her to the invited guest or flicked to some B-roll of the story she was relating. He didn't need to know about another school shooting, or the kittens rescued from a storm drain. Just her. That was all he watched the news for.

Marley Locke. Her soft, sweet features, her dark blonde hair, curling to her shoulders in soft waves, her eyes so full of warmth and empathy.

Those pink lips. The swell of her breasts in the stylish, expensive blouse.

Christ, he wanted her. He'd always wanted her. Ever since that day at college when he'd walked into the library at Harvard and seen her.

No one had come close to her ... ever. With his looks, his

money, his position in New York's Upper East Side, he could have had anyone, and he'd had plenty.

But there was always that one. The one who got away. The girl in the pink T-shirt. The library at the college had been quiet and peaceful. She had been alone in one of the aisles, reading. She'd looked up as he approached. She had been small, slim, and very young, maybe seventeen, eighteen. She had smiled at him. She was lovely, not merely pretty, but achingly beautiful, her large eyes a deep brown, the pink curve of her mouth warm and friendly. Her hair, a dark brown cloud, hanging almost to her waist, had been soft and messy. She had taken his breath away.

She was the one he'd been looking for. He had stepped toward her.

And just like that, she was gone. A voice behind him had called her and she'd smiled her goodbyes and walked past him. Less than thirty seconds, and his life had been forever changed.

AND NOW SHE was on his television every night. This evening, though, things would be different. He knew where to find her; he knew where to take her. His place out in the countryside was secluded and secure. She would learn to love it there.

He opened his eyes as he heard the reporter hand back to Marley. He smiled when he saw her beautiful face again.

Tonight, my darling, tonight ...

MARLEY CLOSED out the news with a smile and waited until the camera told them they were off-air. "Thanks, everyone." She grinned at them as the floor staff clapped her. She was one of the few anchors that treated everyone the same and always was friendly and courteous. Marley laughed off their applause, ignoring her co-anchor when he bitched about them.

Her assistant, Rae, giggled as Marley grabbed her and twirled her around.

"Somebody's in a good mood."

Marley put her friend down and they walked back to her dressing room. "You bet I am. Cory's picking me up and we're going to have two blissful weeks of nothing but sun, sea, sand, and dirty dirty sex."

Rae laughed. "I'm not jealous at all. Really, really not."

Marley chuckled. "I'm sorry, boo. I shouldn't gloat but God, I have been looking forward to this forever."

"Listen, you deserve it. Between you and me? I've been worried that you're working too hard."

"Nah," Marley grinned at her. "You know I live and breathe the news. Listen, while we're sharing secrets ... when I come back, I'm going to ask Jerry if I can take on some more investigative journalism. I love being anchor, but I miss being out in the field too."

Rae smiled at her. She was in her fifties, African-American, and the cream-of-the-cream of personal assistants. She and Marley had clicked immediately on meeting a year ago and had been inseparable since. She chatted with Marley now as Marley changed into jeans and a T-shirt and got ready to meet her boyfriend. She and Cory Wheeler had been together for two years now and were as in love as they had ever been. Marley knew he was the one, his fun-loving and fiercely intelligent personality so matching her in everything they did.

Cory arrived soon after and she kissed him, lingering over the embrace. He grinned down at her, his dark brown eyes merry and excited. "You ready, baby?"

"Lead on, gorgeous man."

They held hands as they walked out of the building to the

waiting cab, and it wasn't until she heard her name being called that Marley turned around to see the man waiting behind them. She began to smile, her automatic response to any fans who waited for her outside the studio.

Then everything seems to slow down, as she saw the gun. She heard Cory's shout, heard the gunshot, saw Cory's chest explode. She screamed her rage as the man leveled the gun at her, and she lunged at him.

Pain.

Her vision went black.

IN THE MORNING, in the hospital, after hours of surgery, they told her. Cory was dead and the man who had killed him and shot her was gone. Missing. In the wind.

And Marley knew she would never feel the warmth of happiness or the feeling of being safe again.

CHAPTER ONE

ne year later ...

MARLEY LOCKE STOPPED EXISTING the moment she closed out the news that night with a smile at her audience and her usual cheery goodbye. She chatted with Rae as usual, changed into her going-home clothes, and told her friend she would see her tomorrow.

Using the stick that she no longer needed, but kept as a way of misdirection, she hobbled out to the waiting town car, and Marley Locke disappeared.

As THE TOWN CAR, driven by one of her FBI handlers, sped out into the dark of New York state and to the safehouse, Marley was forgotten and instead, in her place, Sunday Kemp was 'born.'

At the safehouse, her blonde hair was dyed professionally

back to her original dark brown, her brown eyes covered with violet contact lenses, her nose pierced, even a small tattoo was made on her wrist.

Then, the private jet carrying her to her new home arrived, and she knew this was it. The last moment of her old life. She hesitated once more before stepping onto the aircraft. Sam, her handler, who had become a good friend over the last year, put a hand on her shoulder. "You okay, Sunday?"

Sunday. Her new name. She'd chosen it to honor Cory—they'd met on Sunday. Kemp had been his mother's maiden name. When she'd lost Cory, she'd also lost them. It had been too painful for them to see her, even though Patricia, Cory's mother, had stayed by Marley's bedside as she recovered from the gunshot. As soon as Marley was released, though, she had been on her own. Her own family, long dispersed over the world, had sent commiserations, but not one of them had visited. Rae had been her family, and now she had to leave her only family behind.

From New York, the only home she had ever known, to small-town life in the Rockies. Colorado. From news anchor to someone's typist. They'd found her a position with an artist who lived in the small town near Telluride and she would meet him the following Monday.

Until then, she would be set up in her new home, a small apartment on the main street of the town, high in the Rocky Mountains. She'd brought nothing from home, not even underwear, except for one photograph of Cory that she'd snuck into the lining of her jacket.

The FBI had told her to leave everything that could tie her to her old life. "Everything will be provided for you."

She'd asked them about her money. "You have to leave everything," Sam had told her gently. "You show up in town with millions in the bank …"

"I get it," she'd said. Money hadn't meant anything but making her life more convenient; she'd never been a money-grubber. But she hated leaving her books, her piano, and most of all, her friends at the station.

The threats to her life were constant. He, whoever he was, was relentless but very well-hidden. But he constantly sent her reminders that he was close, that he would finish the job, make her pay for her 'betrayal.'

Asshole. Her gut would churn with anger, and sometimes she wished her stalker would show his face. Even if he killed her, she would at least get her chance for revenge. The FBI were troubled and by the time they'd convinced her that they thought her attacker was someone connected to the Mob and that she would never escape him, Marley—Sunday—had almost resigned herself to dying young.

The FBI, and Sam Duarte, in particular, had finally persuaded her to go into protection. "You have so much more life to live," Sam, a kindly man in his forties, had told her. "You're twenty-eight years old, sweetheart. Live. Live to honor Cory's memory."

He couldn't have put it in any other way that could have persuaded her. Suddenly, a slower pace of life, and the time to grieve for Cory, sounded more tempting than her career and New York.

In the private jet, Sam smiled at her. "You all set, Sunday?"

She nodded. "I think I'm ready now, Sam. Thank you for arranging all of this, I mean it. And the job too. I'd go crazy without something to do."

Sam patted her hand. "I don't know much about your future employer except he keeps himself to himself. Very private."

"Good." She was relieved to hear that. She knew her new

boss had a large house and hoped they wouldn't cross paths that much and that she would be left alone to work and think.

The jet landed in Telluride, then she was given the keys to a secondhand SUV. All part of the ruse, she knew, but she didn't care. It was comfortable and reliable. In the back were suitcases filled with her new wardrobe. Sam made sure she was comfortable. "We'll follow you to the new apartment," he told her, "but keep our distance so we don't attract attention. You look like you've arrived on your own. The place is furnished, so you should be able to settle in pretty quickly. There are a couple of bags of basic groceries in the station wagon. You got the burner phone I gave you?"

Sunday dug in her purse and held it up.

"Good girl. Well, I'll be in touch. Keep that with you, but get a new one to use for your new friends here."

She nodded. "Thank you, Sam."

"You'll be good here, Sunday. I know it."

She drove to the small mountain town of Rockford and down Main Street, parking her car outside the small apartment block and sitting for a time, getting her bearings. She saw, with relief, a small diner, still open even after 1:00 a.m., a gas station and convenience store, brightly lit along the street, and various other small stores. A cute little coffeehouse was on the corner of her block. Yes. She could see herself being settled here.

It didn't take long to unpack. The apartment itself was small but comfortable. The open-plan kitchen and living space had a bay window overlooking Main Street, a small table and chairs nestled into it. A brand-new laptop sat in its box, and Sunday was touched to see that Sam had snuck some of her favorite books onto the bookshelves—not her own well-worn copies, perhaps, but the that fact he'd taken the time to make things homelier for her was a sweet thing to do.

Sunday—her new name really would take some getting used to—unpacked her things and made herself some tea. It was almost 3:00 a.m. by the time she sat down at the small table and gazed out over her new town, but she didn't feel tired at all. Instead, she took a deep breath in ... and burst into tears.

CHAPTER TWO

On the other side of town, her future employer stared at a blank canvas in his studio, seeing in his mind's eye the swirls of color that would cover it, pinks, blues, purples, green, yellow. He could almost reach out and touch the texture of the paint he would load onto his brush.

The piece would be vibrant, exciting ... and he would see very little of it. The colors had started to change a few months back and today, his best friend—and his optometrist—told him why.

He was losing the ability to see color. Him, River Giotto, the wunderkind of the painting world for the last few years, the natural successor to Rothko or Hans Hofmann. Celebrated, feted, and admired and he was losing the colors. The cruelty of it took his breath away.

"Riv?"

River turned to see Luke, his best friend, standing in the doorway of the studio. "I didn't know you were still here."

Luke half-smiled at him. "I was talking to Carmen. She's worried about you. We all are, Riv."

River turned away, not wanting his friend to see the pain in his eyes. "I just need to adjust." He sighed. "Goddamn it, Luke, of all the things to happen."

"I know, buddy. Look, you're only thirty-six, still young. With care and the right treatment, there's no reason you can't ..."

"I'm already losing the colors, Luke. They're not as sharp or as rich." He went to a stack of canvases in the corner of the studio and found what he was looking for. "Look at this. When I painted it, the greens popped, the reds were sumptuous. You know what I see now? Watered down. Faded color. It's not the same painting."

"It is to everyone else, buddy."

River shook his head. "But if I can't express what I want to, paint the way I have, what kind of artist am I? What do I have left?"

Luke took a deep breath in. "River ... I'm going to say this because I'm your best friend, your brother, and I love you. Art ... while it may be a part of you, isn't all you are."

River gave a humorless laugh. "Then why I am I so terrified that it is?"

LATER, when Luke had gone, unable to cheer his friend, River went to his bedroom. The house, a piece of art itself, felt hollow and empty, ringing with silence. His housekeeper, Carmen, no longer stayed at the house at night, wanting to be with her husband, and he couldn't blame her. He hadn't been good company for anyone for he didn't know how long.

River stared back at his reflection. His large, bright green eyes didn't look any different. They had always been his best feature, he thought, and now they were failing him. His dark, shaggy curls were wild about his head, three days of beard on his handsome face. There was a crease between his eyes that, along with his heavy brow, always made him look brooding and unapproachable and, being as reclusive as he was, he'd used that to his benefit.

He'd also used his good looks to sleep with some of the most beautiful women around the world without ever getting too involved. Except one time, and to his chagrin, in that case he'd broken his one rule—never get involved with women in his hometown.

Aria Fielding still lived and worked in Rockford, and although River didn't often go down the hill into town, he still felt bad about the way he had treated her. The sex had been good, but emotionally he had felt nothing. Aria had deserved better, and from what he heard, she still held a grudge about the way things had ended between them, even after almost a year.

Now, since his eyesight had been failing him, myopia as well as the colors fading, he had become more reclusive, by choice. His father, a man River had adored, a second-generation Italian immigrant, had passed ten years ago, fifteen years after River's mother, and had left his billion-dollar fortune to his son, rather than his spiteful, much younger stepmother.

Angelina Marshall-Giotto love to portray herself as a saint. A charity maven in New York, she had wasted no time after her husband's death in trying to seduce his son. River, who had always loathed her, rejected her without thinking twice, and since then Angelina had made it her mission to destroy his life.

His carelessness in sleeping with woman after woman had come back to bite him and Angelina had made sure that everyone found out about his secret daughter.

River had gotten one of his one-night stands pregnant, and Angeline had used that to funnel money from River to herself. Finding out, River had met with the mother of his child and offered her a settlement. Lindsay, the woman, had turned him down. "I don't want your money, River," she'd said coolly. "I want you to know your daughter."

He'd balked but, knowing Angelina would swoop in and turn the girl against him, he'd finally agreed.

The moment he'd met five-year-old Berry, however, his life had changed. The little dark-haired girl stared back at him with clear green eyes, so like his, and River had been lost. Berry was the very best of his world. He and Lindsay had reached an agreement on custody and child support, taking Angelina out of the loop once and for all.

His one regret was that Berry lived in Phoenix most of the time. It had been on her last visit to him that he'd begun to notice the changes in his eyes. She had been wearing a little dress that he'd brought back from Paris. The flowers on it, which had been a vivid mix of red, oranges, and pinks, to his eye suddenly looked faded. He'd frowned. "I guess your mom has to wash that a lot, huh?"

Berry, already precocious, completely confident in front of her father, shook her head. "No, I only wear it on special occasions, Daddy."

River had brushed the matter aside, putting it down to his memory, but later, when his paintings had begun to change, he had known it was something serious.

RIVER LEANED his head against the cool glass of his window and closed his eyes. I have to get out of this funk, he thought. Berry needed him. Luke, Carmen ... he would have to try to make the best of his situation, even if his heart was breaking. He sighed and went to bed.

THE NEXT MORNING, Sunday woke, freezing cold and stiff. Groaning, she rolled out of bed and felt the radiator. Cold. Dammit. Her lower back ached—the bullet had smashed into it and was still lodged there—and she felt a wave of nausea at the pain. It was always worse in the cold.

She cranked the heating up to full and made herself some tea while she waited for the apartment to warm up. In New York, things like that had always been taken care of for her.

She grinned to herself. Talk about entitlement. Sunday pulled the comforter around her as she drank her tea and soon enough, her new home was warming up.

It was still early, just after dawn, and when she could face going to the window, she looked out onto the streets of the small town. It looked quaint, even old-fashioned, to her Manhattan eyes, but she could see from the lines of stores and businesses that it was a working town, not as flashy as its near neighbor, Telluride. She'd never been to Colorado before and the sight of the mountains, the snow, the pine forests was almost magical to her.

It was February, and the snow lay in thick drifts at the sides of the street. Even this early, some people were clearing the sidewalks, sprinkling salt or kitty litter down on the ground. Nothing got in the way of the business here. She saw a tall, pale white young woman emerged from the coffeehouse on the corner, her long dark hair flying as she skidded on the icy ground. Sunday grinned as she saw the girl laugh, her head thrown back as she clung to the streetlight nearest to her. Sunday heard some men calling out to the girl, saw two local deputies going to her aid, watched as the girl laughed with them and beckoned them into the coffeehouse.

She looked so free, so relaxed. Sunday made up her mind to go to the coffeehouse as soon as she was dressed and say hello. The girl looked approachable and fun.

Luckily, in the shower, she took care to wait until the water ran warm before stepping into it. Once in, Sunday shampooed her dark hair then let the water soothe her aching body. The bed was little more than a makeshift cot, and she resolved to buy herself a proper bed as soon as she could afford it.

Which was weird. In her New York account sat nearly two million dollars ... and she couldn't touch it. Her credit cards, were all destroyed now. The FBI had given her a certain amount to survive on while she earned her first paycheck and waited for new credit cards in her new name, but it would only be enough for food and rent.

Jesus, she thought now as she dried her hair, all of this because of one asshole's obsession. A whole life erased. She felt a jolt of guilt. At least you have a life to be changed, Marley Locke. What about Cory?

She dug the photograph of him out of her jacket and traced the shape of his face. God, I miss you, baby. I'm so sorry, so, so, sorry. She could feel tears threatening again but dashed them away with an impatient hand. No. No more wallowing.

OUTSIDE, the temperature was below freezing and big clouds of her breath almost fogged her vision. Sunday tottered uncertainly along the sidewalk, smiling shyly at people who said hello to her, hoping no one would recognize her. Without her signature blonde hair, without the carefully applied makeup, she doubted it. She had, after all, decided against the violet contact lenses. She hated the feel of the things and besides, she mused to herself, her brown eyes were nothing remarkable, especially without makeup.

She pushed her way into the Lumia coffeehouse to be greeted by a wave of chatter. Clearly, everyone in Rockford gathered here, and for a moment, she almost thought about turning around and escaping.

But then the girl she had seen this morning appeared in front of her with a wide smile. "'Allo," she said in a broad English accent, "You're new here, ain't you?"

Sunday grinned back at her. The woman's smile was huge, infectious, and friendly. "I am. Hello, I'm Sunday."

She held out her hand, and the other woman balanced a tray on her other arm and shook it. "Hello, sweets, I'm Daisy. Nice to meet you. Want some coffee?"

"Please."

"Come and sit at the counter with me and I'll give you all the gossip."

She followed Daisy back to the counter, nodding politely at some curious customers. Daisy was resplendent in a red dress which clung to breakneck curves, her almost-black hair tumbling in waves down her back. Even at eight in the morning, Daisy had applied bright red lipstick, which only enhanced her thousand-watt smile.

"What's your poison?"

Sunday settled on the stool at the counter and looked at the beverage list. "I'd kill for just a huge mug of black coffee."

"My favorite too," Daisy said easily and poured out a steaming cup for Sunday. "Here. Now, welcome to Rockford." She studied Sunday as she sipped her own coffee too. "You here with family?"

Sunday nodded. Here we go. The questions she and Sam had practiced until she was word perfect. The lies. The fake histories. "No, just for work. Time from a change from California."

They'd decided on California because of the accent. She could pull that off easily. Daisy rolled her eyes, grinning. "Yes, a break from all that sun sounds like heaven."

Sunday smiled. "Seriously, when there is no change of

season for years on end, it gets a little wearying. So, I decided to come here. It's beautiful." That wasn't a lie, at least.

Daisy nodded. "It is, I'll give it that."

"You're obviously not from these parts."

"How d'you guess?" Daisy chuckled. "My dad met my stepmum in London, but she had to come back here. She was the daughter of the owner of the old ski place up the mountain so when he died, she had to run it. So me and Dad moved over to the States."

"You like it?"

"I do, actually. It was so different to me, the whole culture, but I've been here nearly half my life now, twelve years. I'm used to it." Daisy nodded at her coffee. "It'll get cold."

The coffee was smooth and rich. "God, that's good."

"I thank you." Daisy did a small curtsy which made Sunday laugh. She warmed to the woman instantly. "So, what do you do?"

"I'm a copywriter and transcriber. I'm here to work for River Giotto, transcribing his father's journals."

Daisy stopped and a wary look came into her eyes. "Really?"

Sunday nodded, her interest piqued. "Is that notable?"

Daisy shook herself. "No, no, just a little surprising. River is a little reclusive. I'm surprised he's allowing a stranger—no offense—into his home. You know where he lives, right?"

"Kind of. I mean, I have an address."

Daisy made a signal for her to wait and disappeared into the backroom. A second later she emerged and waved an iPad at her. "Look."

She turned the tablet towards Sunday so she could see. Sunday gave a gasp. The house—was it even right to call it a mere house? —was magnificent, set by a lake and surrounded by mountains. A sprawling single-level home which almost seemed to be made entirely from glass, it had clean lines and a simplicity to it which belied the majesty of the place. Daisy flicked to a photograph of it lit up at night, reflected back at itself in the surrounding lake.

Sunday could feel herself boggling at it and knew Daisy was gauging her reaction. "It's beautiful."

"Isn't it? We tend to call it 'The Castle' but in truth, we're all slavering to own something like that. River can afford it, of course."

"What's he like?"

Daisy considered. "For an old dude, he's okay. Very handsome, very rich. Listen," she leaned in closely, "my stepsister, aka 'the dragon,' used to date him so don't mention him around her."

"Mention who?"

Daisy sighed as the voice came from behind her. Sunday saw a diminutive, but staggeringly beautiful woman behind them. Her hair was cut short, close to her head, and her face was utterly exquisite, and her dark brown eyes were piercing as she looked at Sunday with a distinct lack of friendliness. "Who's this?"

"Ari, this is Sunday, my new friend. She just moved here. Sunday, this is the Dragon, or Aria, as we sometimes call her when she's being nice. Which is rare." Daisy grinned easily at her stepsister, who scowled at her. Aria slipped out of her coat, and Sunday saw she had the athletic body of a dancer. Something clicked in Sunday's brain.

"You're Aria Fielding."

Both Daisy and Aria stopped. Aria studied Sunday. "You know me?"

"You used to dance at NYSMBC ... under Grace Hardacre."

Aria's eyes were flinty. "You know ballet?"

Sunday shook her head and cursed inwardly. "Not a lot. A

cousin I was staying in New York with took me to a performance. You were wonderful."

There was no discernible thawing in Aria's attitude; if anything, she seemed even frostier now. "Thank you." The words were stiff, and she soon walked away from them.

Daisy sighed. "Sorry about her. She's, um, difficult."

"Artistic temperament," Sunday said, patting her new friend's hand and Daisy smiled at her gratefully.

"You're a sweetheart. Listen, if you need anything, any help to settle in, you're always welcome. I know all the best maintenance guys or the best stuff at the farmer's market—avoid the cheese counter. Seriously. Go into Telluride for your dairy cravings."

Sunday chuckled. "I'll remember that. I guess I'll just take a drive around, get my bearings."

"Come and have supper with me tomorrow night," Daisy said. "I'm not much of a chef but I can rustle up some pasta."

"I'd like that, thank you." The weight of her new life was already lifting, thanks to this sweet English girl. They arranged a time and Sunday thanked her again.

SHE FOUND the farmer's market and shopped for a week's worth of groceries, avoiding the cheese counter as Daisy had advised. Feeling restless and not wanting to spend all day alone in the apartment, she flicked her phone onto GPS mode and decided to go check out her future employer's place.

She drove up the mountainside carefully, cringing a little at the sheer drop on one side, imagining her SUV crashing through the pine trees and exploding. Dramatic, much? She chuckled to herself and concentrated on the road ahead. Soon enough, she was turning into a long driveway.

She parked a little way from the house, not wanting to

intrude, but she could see from here that the photographs of the place didn't do it justice. She felt a pang of sadness—Cory, one of New York's up-and-coming architects, would have loved this place. Not only was the design out of the world, but the tranquility here, the peace, was breathtaking.

She heard another vehicle coming up the hill behind her and got back into her station wagon guiltily. She smoothed her face into a bland smile as the car pulled up beside hers. A pleasant young man smiled at her as he rolled down his window. "Hey, you lost?"

"I'm fine," she said, feeling her face burn. He had kind hazel eyes and a sweet smile. "I'm just checking out my new job."

His eyes lit up. "Oh, are you Sunday?"

Was this River Giotto? No, surely not. This man seemed far too outgoing to be a reclusive artist. He seemed to read her mind. He got out of his car and shook her hand. "Luke Maslany. I'm River's friend, for my sins."

"Sunday Kemp. Honestly, I didn't mean to intrude or pry, I was just getting my bearings. Ready for Monday morning, you know?" She was rambling in her embarrassment, but this guy had the nicest smile.

"Listen, why not get a proper jump? Come up to the house. Carmen will be there—River's housekeeper. You'll probably see more of her than anyone. We might even be able to persuade River to show his face."

Sunday hesitated. She had no makeup on, her hair was a mess ... did she really want to make this first impression? "I think maybe I should wait until Monday. I don't want to intrude."

Luke Maslany nodded, but his eyes crinkled when he smiled and Sunday couldn't help but like him. "Listen, entirely up to you, but I know for a fact that Carmen is making brunch, and she always makes a ton. River barely eats, so I," and he patted his flat stomach, "get the guilts on his behalf and end up stuffed. You'd be doing me a favor."

Sunday laughed. He was so charming ... and once again she found herself marveling at the friendliness of these people. "Well, if you promise I'm not imposing."

"Of course not. Shall we?"

3
CHAPTER THREE

River felt a jolt of annoyance at the knock on the door but kept his voice level. "Come in."

Luke poked his head around the door and grinned at his friend. "Hey, dude."

"Hey, Luke." Even in his glum mood, River was always happy to see Luke. "You come to Carmel's feast?"

"Of course—and I brought a guest."

"Oh?" River couldn't have been less interested. He rarely joined Carmel and Luke in the kitchen, preferring to eat alone in his studio.

"Your new employee."

"The typist?"

"The transcriber," Luke said with a tone in his voice. "Don't think she'd be impressed with being described as a typist."

River shrugged. "Whatever. Carmel hired her. She'll tell her what to do, where to go."

"Come meet her, Riv," Luke said, and he sounded weary, as if he was tired of being the intermediary on River's behalf. "She'll be here five days a week, all hours. You'll meet her sometime."

"Then I'll meet her sometime." River knew he was being

obtuse, but he really wasn't in the mood for pleasantries. Lindsay had called him this morning, asking him if he could take Berry for a few weeks for some unknown reason, and although River had agreed, and looked forward to seeing his daughter, he was irritated that possibly his final days of being able to paint the way River Giotto painted would be even more limited.

He was in no mood to meet anyone and nothing Luke could say to change his mind. Luke left him alone, clearly pissed, but River sighed with relief. He continued painting, and yet from the other side of the house, he could hear laughter and chatter and felt the weight of loneliness. He could smell the delicious scent of one of Carmel's signature curries filling the house and felt his mouth water. He knew she would leave him some leftovers in the refrigerator. He put down his paintbrush and wiped his hands. Barefoot as ever, he padded silently through the house to the guest bedroom. The window there looked out over the kitchen and he could watch them unseen.

He saw Carmen fussing around the breakfast counter, talking to a young woman with waist-length dark hair. River watched her as she moved around the kitchen to help Carmel, the way her body moved, almost like a dancer, graceful and strong. River narrowed his eyes to see her features and felt his groin tighten.

She was lovely. Truly a beautiful young woman. Her features were soft, kind, a faint blush on her olive skin, her smile wide. She was about five-five, a foot shorter than River's six-five, and slim but curvy. He watched her chat easily to Carmen, joke around with Luke, and wondered who the hell this woman was. She was stunning, but did he really need stunning in his life?

No. Hell, no. He'd stay away from her, take her out of the equation, concentrate on Berry, and on his eyesight. Despite what Luke had told him, there had to be something, somewhere in the world, which could help him.

Because otherwise what was the point? It was too cruel. He looked back at his newest employee one last time and wondered if she'd even known true despair. He doubted it.

River turned away from the sight of his friends enjoying each other and went back to his lonely studio.

SUNDAY PUT a hand over her stomach and protested as Carmen packed two large plastic boxes with curry. "I can't, you've spoiled me enough."

"Nonsense. You just moved in; you need feeding. Take it." Carmen grinned at her. She and Sunday had clicked straight away. "You need a taste of home."

Sunday smiled at her. Carmen was a second-generation Indian American and when Sunday had told her that her own grandmother hailed from Kerala, it had sealed Carmen's approval of Sunday herself. "I've never been to India," Sunday told her, "it was one of those things that ..." She stopped. She was about to say it was one of those things she and Cory had planned to do, possibly for their honeymoon. "I just never got around to it."

"There's still time," Carmen said, shrugging. "You're what, twenty-five?"

"Twenty-eight."

"Gah, plenty of time. So, we'll see you again on Monday?"

Sunday smiled. "You will. Bright and early."

She hugged Carmen, feeling as if they had known each other for ever. Luke, too, was easy to talk to, and he walked her back to her car. "I'm sorry about River. He's an ornery pain in the ass, but he'll come around."

Sunday shrugged good-naturedly. "Hey, as long as I do my work and I get paid, it's no bother to me."

Luke shook her hand, and she was strangely touched by his old-fashioned manners. "Good luck with the job," he said to her, "I can already tell you're going to fit in with us. Some of us, anyway," he added with a grin. "You can find your way back into town okay?"

"I can, thanks. And thanks again for inviting me in. You're right, it will make it easier to start work."

"Good. See you around."

BY THE TIME she drove back into town, just after lunchtime, the light was already fading, snow clouds making the sky a riot of purple, pink, and black. As Sunday carried her bags of groceries and the plastic boxes of curry into her apartment, she reflected that in just a few hours, she had made—if not yet friends—certainly people with the potential to be friends. Daisy. Carmen. Luke.

She read for most of the rest of the day, falling asleep on the couch—a couch, she noted, that was vastly more comfortable than her bed—and waking to see thick, fluffy snow falling. She sat at the window for hours just watching it fall, listening to the silence, the peace. The streetlamps struggled to illuminate the main road through the snow. Sunday shook her head, chuckling softly to herself. It was like a dreamland, a Christmas fairy tale, not real life.

And yet, this was her real life now and for the first time since that terrible night where she'd lost everything, lost Cory, lost the life she had planned for, had worked for, the former Marley Locke felt hope.

. . .

When his man reported back that Marley hadn't been home at all for the entire weekend, Brian Scanlan was irked but not surprised. "She thinks she can hide from me," he shrugged, as his employees listened to him. There was an air of nervousness in the room, as if the other men were waiting for Brian's temper to explode. But tonight, he felt magnanimous.

Let Marley think she'd escape him, that she wasn't still alive merely because he'd allowed her to be. That night, a year ago, when his hitman had taken out the boyfriend—as he'd been ordered to—and shot Marley—which he had been explicitly told not to—Brian had known that next time, he would do the deed himself. He couldn't risk her getting away again and she'd made his planning easier by not skipping town after she'd been released from hospital.

But then again—where the hell would she run to? He knew better than anyone that she had no one. Her family was scattered; her boyfriend's family would blame her for his murder. She had friends, yes. But he'd been right—Marley had stayed put, albeit with increased security.

As if that would stop him. No one even suspected the great Brian Scanlan, doyen of the Upper East Side, to have such close ties with the Mob, let alone be a stone-cold killer. The man he'd hired to kill Cory Wheeler was himself now dead—a punishment for hurting Brian's love. The night he'd found that Marley was in the hospital with a gunshot wound to the belly ... no. Only he would decide whether she lived or died. She belonged to him, and no other.

He'd been magnanimous long enough, giving her time to grieve for her lost love, but now it was time. He'd made the arrangements over the past year—a new apartment for them to live in together on the Upper East Side, a whole new wardrobe for Marley, each piece tailored just for her in the colors that he, Brian, had approved. He'd make her dye her hair back to its natural color—she looked like a whore with that blonde mess. Make her scrub the makeup from her beautiful face—the mother of his children would not need it.

Yes, he had everything planned for her, and now it was time to put that plan into action.

It was only the next morning, when Marley failed to appear on his television screen, that Brian Scanlan discovered that he had been wrong. Marley had escaped him.

Marley was gone.

And his rage knew no limits.

CHAPTER FOUR

Monday morning, Sunday tried to put the fact that she was gone from New York would today become public and tried to concentrate on the drive up to the Giotto house. The night before, she'd spent a fun evening with Daisy Nash, and now she was full of optimism that her job would be just what she was looking for.

Carmen greeted her like an old friend and showed her to the little office where Sunday found a state-of-the-art laptop set up for her, as well as a comfortable chair and solid oak desk. A couch completed the room, of which one wall was solid glass looking out over the valley below.

Sunday shook her head, chuckling in disbelief. "How am I supposed to concentrate in the face of that?" She indicated the view and Carmen smiled.

"You'll do fine. Listen, anything you need, come find me and please help yourself to anything in the kitchen, food, drink. You have a mini-fridge with water and sodas, but anything else, please, really, help yourself." Carmen glanced at her watch. "I'll do lunch for one o'clock, okay?"

"I wouldn't want to impose."

Carmen rolled her eyes, smiling. "See you later. Oh, bathroom at the end of the corridor on the right."

Sunday sat down at the desk and pulled her reading glasses from her bag. Two fat journals sat at the side of the desk—presumably the ones Giotto wanted transcribed. She wondered why he hadn't done it himself but when she opened them, she realized why. The handwriting was neat but incredibly tiny, the script beautifully rendered. Instantly Sunday knew this would be the work of months rather than weeks and she was relieved. She'd wondered how on earth transcribing two diaries could take more than a few weeks, at least, but now, seeing the thickness of the books and the writing that covered every page? Yeah, she'd be okay for a few months.

She flicked on the laptop, saw it was set up with every piece of software she could hope for, and spent an hour or two setting it up the way she liked it. Then she took one of the journals and sat on the couch to read through the first few entries, curling her legs up under her and winding her hair up into a bun.

She soon got absorbed into the diary. Ludovico Giotto had been a man of vision, of incredible intelligence and warmth, that much was obvious even from the first few pages. They dated back almost fifty years to when Ludo's father had brought his young wife to America to begin their family. Already a billionaire, Giovanni Giotto had doted on his four children, especially his eldest, Ludo, but had also been determined they would have the best of everything only when they had learned to appreciate it. He had sent them to prestigious colleges on the understanding that, afterward, they would all give five years of their lives to voluntary service. All of them, except his daughter Perdita, had fulfilled their promise. Perdita, Ludo's adored youngest sibling, had never lived to go to college, succumbing to tuberculosis when she was eight.

Ludo, and his surviving sisters had worked even harder after that, and not only had given their promised five years but extended that promise to their future spouses and children.

We all lived lives of great privilege, Ludo wrote, but none of us ever took it for granted. We saw many among our peers and our father's peers who lost everything and had no way to pull themselves up, for they had never witnessed or experienced true hardship. We, at least, knew nothing in this world is certain, and certainly nothing we had in material worth meant anything in the long run.

"True story," Sunday murmured to herself and looked up from the book, rolling her neck. Her journalistic senses were tingling in a way they hadn't for a long, long time and she wondered idly if River Giotto would allow her to work on an official biography of his father and his family.

She closed the book and went to the computer. Opening up a browser window, she paused. Monday. The first day that Marley Locke officially didn't show up for work. Would it be torturous to see if her absence had made any news? That's presumptuous, she thought, shaking her head. No. Behind the scenes they would be wondering, even worrying, but nothing would be said on screen until it had to be.

And then ... God, she could barely even think about the lengths the FBI had gone to protect her. An unidentified Jane Doe matching her description. Someone's daughter, someone's baby, would be used as a decoy. Someone from the police would 'identify' the body as Marley's. A suicide. Or an accident. Marley Locke would be officially dead.

Sunday shivered. What a life. She stood up and stretched, closing the laptop. She didn't need to know what was going on in New York, it would just upset her. Focus on your job.

At lunchtime, she shyly went to the kitchen and Carmen waved a spatula at her as she hovered around the stove. "We're having omelets. I hope that's okay? His majesty isn't eating, so it's just the two of us."

For some reason, Sunday felt relieved. After reading River's father's diary, she felt as if she would want to pepper the man with questions, and it really wasn't an appropriate time for that.

Carmen flipped a stunning-looking omelet onto a plate for her. "It's just veggie—we have meat-free Mondays here, much to River's disgust. But it keeps him just a little healthier."

"He likes his meat?"

"He does. Red meat, red wine, cigarettes. That's River's fuel. Thankfully, I've banned smoking in the main house."

Sunday giggled. "You really are the boss."

"I have to be. River takes artistic temperament to the nth degree." Carmen's smile faded. "But he's going through a hard time at the moment, so I'll let him rant and rave if he wants to."

She didn't offer any further information and Sunday didn't feel as if she had the right to pry. They chatted happily while they ate their lunch, Sunday complimenting the chef on the light, fluffy omelets. She finished it all to Carmen's approval.

"Good girl."

"I'm never one to say no to food."

"Favorite?"

Sunday considered. "A good flame-grilled steak and a bloomin' onion. God, onions. I can be summoned by someone just frying them near me."

Carmen laughed. "Then I'll remember that."

Sunday thanked her for lunch again and went back to her office, feeling happy. If this was to be her life now, then she felt blessed. Going back to the chapters she had read, she began to transcribe them onto the computer, and by the time she looked up from her work, it was dark outside. She stared at her reflection in the window. She saw sad eyes, dark hair escaping from the messy bun, the tiny glint of the nose stud in her ear. She had to admit, she looked nothing like the polished news anchor she had been only a few days ago, but in a strange way, she felt she looked more like herself.

Just after seven, she packed her bag and walked through the house to say goodbye to Carmen. As she walked into the kitchen, she saw a movement out of the corner of her eye and turned to look out of the window. Across the courtyard, the far wing of the house stood mostly in darkness. Was she imagining it or was there a figure silhouetted against the black, watching her?

Sunday squinted. Yes. He was there ... somehow, she knew it was her mysterious employer. Feeling awkward, she raised her hand halfway in greeting then let it drop. Weirdo. She turned and walked away from the kitchen, running into Carmen in the driveway and bidding her goodbye for the evening, without mentioning the incident.

THE APARTMENT WAS cold again and Sunday decided that, while the heating did its job, she would go out to eat supper. There was a diner along the block and, gratefully, she huddled down into a corner booth.

A young, punky-looking waitress whose nametag read Cleo came over. "What can I get you?"

Sunday scanned the plastic menu quickly. "Oh, um, black coffee and a ... um ..."

Cleo grinned at her suddenly. "I'll give you a minute, honey, don't worry. Nice tattoo. I'll get your coffee."

Sunday smiled her thanks at her. Really, people were so nice. The place was pretty full, obviously a favorite haunt of the locals, and when later on, Cleo brought Sunday a stacked burger and fries, Sunday could understand why. She moaned as the savory burger juices hit her taste buds, and the salty, hot fries crunch satisfyingly under her teeth.

One good thing about not being on camera anymore, she thought with a grin to herself, is no more calorie restrictions. She had warm apple pie for dessert and then groaned as Cleo offered her a second helping on the house. "God, no, that's so kind, but I will actually explode."

Cleo grinned. "Daisy said you were nice. We're buddies."

"That makes sense. I hope we will be too."

"Right back atcha." Cleo looked around to see if her manager was watching then slipped into the seat opposite Sunday. "Listen, just a quick word of warning, friend to friend. Daisy tells me you're working for River?"

Sunday nodded. Cleo sighed. "Then watch out for Aria. Daisy won't say this, but Aria's a grade-A bitch. She'll make trouble for you if she can. Ignore it."

"I will, thanks. Not here to make any enemies."

Cleo grinned at her. "You are nice. Hey-ho, boss is back. Listen, let's have coffee soon, yes? Not here, I mean."

"I'd love to."

SUNDAY LINGERED OVER HER COFFEE, not wanting to leave the warmth of the diner. Cleo, having finished her shift, had left a half hour before and Sunday had made sure she got the generous tip she had certainly earned.

Cleo had thanked her and left her cell phone number. "For whenever or whatever," she'd said.

Sunday was reading news stories on her cellphone when she heard someone come into the rapidly-emptying diner. She looked up and saw a man, tall, with shaggy dark curls, brush snow off of his coat. He glanced across at her and their eyes locked.

Sunday felt a jolt through her entire body. The man was spectacular looking, a ruggedly handsome face, but it was his eyes that got her. Light green and thickly rimmed by black lashes, they gazed at her without wavering. She felt that glance everywhere.

Time seemed to freeze but then he walked over to her booth. "May I?"

Oh, darn it. Why did he have to have that deep, sexy, gravelly voice too? She nodded dumbly. He sat down opposite her. Another waitress drifted over and took his order for black coffee. He looked at Sunday questioningly.

She shook her head. "Just one, please."

Sunday felt like a lovestruck teenager and she cleared her throat, trying to stop her face from burning.

"You're new here." A statement, not a question, but she nodded anyway.

"Sund—"

"No names."

A thrill of something shot through her and suddenly she knew that whatever was going on here, she was going to let happen. She wanted this man, whoever he was, and she didn't need complications. A one-night stand? Yes, please. She let the desire show in her eyes and his mouth hitched up in a satisfied smile.

His arrogance was compelling and strangely sexy and Sunday grinned back at him. "You're very confident."

"I know what I want."

"And what's that?"

"You. I don't like to mess around or play games."

"Me neither." Sunday straightened her back. "Nor do I want complications."

"Then we agree. Do you have a place nearby?"

"Yes."

He tilted his head onto one side. "Are you're sure about this?"

"Like I said, no complications. You want to fuck? Let's fuck." Sunday couldn't quite believe the words were coming out of her own mouth, but what the hell? New life, new rules. The last thing she wanted was a relationship with anyone, but her body had needs, for chrissakes.

Her suitor gazed at her for a long moment, then grabbed her hand, pulling her to her feet. "Let's go, beautiful."

CHAPTER FIVE

They ran through the snow to her apartment. Inside, he drew her close and crushed his lips against hers. God, he tasted good. She snaked her hand down and cupped his cock through his jeans. Huge. She moaned in anticipation and he chuckled.

"That's all for you, beautiful. Now get your clothes off."

They stripped each other quickly, tumbling onto her bed. His body was hard and well-muscled, broad shoulders leading down to slim hips and strong legs. He ran his hands over her body, admiration clear in his eyes. "Sensational," he murmured, then bent his head to take her nipple into his mouth.

"Wait ... wait ... I don't have any protection ..."

Without breaking contact with her breast, he leaned over and grabbed his jeans, pulling a condom out of his back pocket. Sunday relaxed, closing her eyes as his tongue flicked around her nipple, sending sweet sensations through her body.

Sunday stroked his long, thick cock against her belly, feeling it quiver and tremble under her touch, swelling in her hand. "You keep doing that, gorgeous, and I'll have to fuck you before I do anything else."

Sunday grinned at him and began to stroke harder. He groaned. "God, you dirty little girl ..."

She tore the condom packet open and rolled it down his cock as he hitched her legs around his waist. "You're gonna take this all, pretty girl."

He thrust into her and Sunday almost screamed at the pure animal pleasure of it. They fucked hard, each clawing and biting at the other, kissing until their mouths were sore. God, it felt so good be fucked without inhibition, to know there were no feelings involved, to be this animal, this feral, this abandoned.

Eventually their fucking grew so rough, they tumbled to the floor, and he pinned her hands above her head as he drove her towards a body-shattering orgasm.

Sunday came hard, her back arching up, her belly pressing against his. A year's worth of pent-up emotion poured out of her and tears streamed down her face as she cried out. Embarrassed, she turned her head away from him but he gently kissed them away without saying anything.

They lay side by side, panting, then, not needing words, they made love again, slowly, exploring the other's body. She loved how his body was so much bigger than hers, his arms thickly banded with muscles cradling her as if she was the most precious thing in the world. She stroked her fingers down his face—he was so beautiful, he didn't seem real—seeing the trouble in his eyes and wondering about it.

But, no. Don't wonder that. Don't wonder about him. Keep this as what it is... a wonderful, sensual, spectacular interlude. She pressed her lips to his, wanting to remember every inch of him because she knew in her heart—this was a one-time thing.

They made love into the early hours before Sunday was unable to keep her eyes open a moment longer.

In the morning, he was gone.

. . .

IN THE SHOWER, Sunday flexed her muscles and felt the delicious ache of the recently fucked. Her thighs throbbed; her vagina was raw from the pounding of her lover's huge cock. There were faint bite marks on her breasts, her shoulders. Her mouth was still tingling from his kiss.

And inside her, something had been released. Something she hadn't known was there, a block. The lack of intimacy since Cory's murder hadn't been something she had thought about, but now, after last night, she realized how distant, physically, she had kept everyone else for the last year.

She drove up to the Giotto house, taking some fresh bread from the town bakery for Carmen, who thanked her and invited her to share a coffee with her. "I have some news. Not that it will directly affect you, but you should know."

She indicated the stool and Sunday sat, watching her new friend curiously. "What's up?"

"Well, River's daughter will be coming to stay for a few weeks, is all, and Berry is adorable, but a handful."

"Mr. Giotto has a daughter?"

"Five years old, but he's only known her for a few years. I believe she was the product of a one-night stand."

Sunday hoped her face wasn't as red as it felt. "It happens. So, Berry—and what a great name, huh?—she's coming to stay for a few weeks?"

Carmen nodded. "River has promised me that he'll do most of the heavy lifting, but I know him. There will be days when he's in his studio and he forgets about everything, including Berry. Those days you might find yourself with a little helper."

"I don't mind that, as long as Mr. Giotto understands I'll be distracted from work."

Carmen grinned. "You can call him River, you know."

"Do you think I'll ever meet him?" Sunday had already imagined what he'd look like—gray-haired, grumpy. Daisy had said he was 'old,' but then Daisy was twenty-four. 'Old' could mean anyone over thirty.

Carmen sighed. "I hope so, sweetheart, I do. I know this might seem a strange situation to you but River has never been a very sociable person. He got worse after his mother died and his father remarried." She lowered her voice. "His stepmother is a vile, vicious woman. Something happened between her and River and he was never the same."

"God, how awful."

Carmen nodded. "He would never tell anyone what happened, but it must have been pretty bad. He had bruises, but he wouldn't tell his father."

"How old was he when this happened?"

"Sixteen. It's been twenty years and he still won't talk about it."

So 'old' was thirty-six? Sunday blinked, adjusting her image of her enigmatic employer. "That's just awful. Is she still around?"

"Unfortunately, but thankfully, she lives in New York. She'd better not show her face here anytime soon."

Sunday nodded, and soon she went back to her office to start work. She couldn't stop thinking about what Carmel had told her and wondered if Ludovico'd had any idea his son was being abused by his wife. Sunday shook her head, angry for River. She had no time for men or women who abused kids. She gave into temptation and typed Ludo's name into a search engine. She found pictures of a handsome, silver-haired man with a much younger woman—a woman Sunday recognized immediately. "No fucking way," she hissed under her breath.

Angelina freaking Marshall. The Wicked Witch of the Upper East Side. Sunday smiled grimly. Suddenly, the abuse didn't seem so surprising. Angelina was both feared and reviled, but her money, her position as the daughter of one of New York's most powerful families, meant people fawned around her, regardless. Sunday or rather, Marley, had interviewed the woman once for a segment on the early show and had disliked her immensely. She'd nicknamed Angelina 'Our Lady of Perpetual Victimhood' after the woman had claimed to have suffered from several serious illnesses without any evidence of such poor health. When Marley had called her out on air, she'd made an enemy of the other woman. Angelina had called Marley's boss, demanding Marley be fired. Jack, the station owner, had refused point blank. They didn't pander to people like Angelina Marshall.

Now, Sunday wondered if Ludo had written about his ex-wife. She flicked through the diaries but found they stopped before River's mother had died. Sunday chewed her lip. On a hunch, she went to find Carmen and asked her if there were more diaries.

"Oh yes, honey, there'll be a few more volumes. River told me to give you a couple at a time so you didn't feel overwhelmed."

"Gotcha."

"Any reason you asked?"

Yes. I know Angelina Marshall. "No, just wondered, as the two you gave me seem to only got to a certain date."

Carmen wiped her hands. "Come with me." She led her through the house and into a large study. "Now, don't judge, but this is Ludo's study. Not his actual study, you understand, but River had it copied exactly when he had the house built. Over here."

She pointed to a bookcase that reached from floor to ceiling. Sunday almost moaned with happiness when she saw it. It looked a little like the library from Beauty and the Beast. She ran a flat hand over the spines of the books. "Heaven."

Carmen chuckled. "I knew you were hiding your inner geek.

River's the same about libraries. I'm sure he wouldn't mind if you want to borrow anything. And if you want more of Ludo's diaries, have at them."

Carmen left her to enjoy the library at her leisure. Sunday hoisted a few of Ludo's diaries out and bore them back to her office. Her interest was piqued now, and she searched through them until she found the first mention of Angelina. Settling on the couch, she read for a few hours. The day soon went and although she had read nearly a whole journal, she had found nothing out of the ordinary. She marveled at Ludo's attention to detail, though—the man documented everything except his bathroom habits, she found, and yet it was never boring. She decided she would have liked to know Ludovico Giotto very much. He was warm and humorous and obviously adored his first wife and his son.

Carmen had told her that today was her half-day off and so, at suppertime, Sunday packed her bag and walked through the silent house. There was something both comforting yet charged about the silence of the house. Outside, she stood for a moment, listening to the faint sound of snow falling and breathed in a lungful of the freezing air. Yes, she could get used to this peace.

Once again, the feeling of being watched came over her. She looked toward the far end of the house and smiled. "Why don't you come talk to me?" she said out loud, out into the silence, but there was no answer. *Who are you?* "Whatever she did to you, I'd like to make her pay for it." Sunday said that softly, to herself.

Even after everything had happened to her, she still went out, made new friends, had experiences. She could not imagine being so scarred by something that she would disappear into exile.

Isn't that just what you've done though?

Not by choice.

Sunday got into her truck and drove back into town. She saw the coffeehouse was still open and stopped to say hi to Daisy.

Her friend seemed delighted to see her. "Hiya. Americano?"

"I'm in the mood for hot chocolate, actually. I need the sugar."

Daisy grinned and nodded to a chair. "Grab a pew. I'll bring it over."

Sunday sat, dumping her purse on the floor next to her. She nodded at Aria, who smiled blandly but didn't come over. She was talking to a handsome young man with dark blond hair and blue eyes, who looked at Sunday with interest. Aria murmured something to him and they both laughed, and Sunday felt her face flush. What was this, ninth grade?

Daisy brought over two cups of hot chocolate and sat down, flashing an annoyed glance at her stepsister. "Ignore her," she told Sunday, "she never grew up. So, how's things? Settling in? Met River yet?"

Sunday smiled at her new friend. "Good. Yes and no. The mysterious Mr. Giotto remains a stranger. I did meet Cleo at the diner last night." For some reason, she didn't want to mention the delectable stranger whom she had taken home. That was for her alone, her dirty little secret.

Daisy was grinning. "I love Cleo. She's so effortlessly cool. I'm a dork and yet she still decided I was to be her best friend. She's from New York, you know?"

"I didn't." A small curl of unease started in Sunday's stomach—would Cleo recognize her? Daisy didn't notice her disquiet.

"Well, anyway, so the job is going okay? I'm not surprised River's hiding out."

"What's he like? I know he's thirty-six and an artist but that's all I know." Sunday knew she shouldn't be pumping Daisy for information, that she was drawing on their tentative friendship, but she couldn't help herself. Since finding out about River's stepmother ... she felt she had to know more.

"Gorgeous-looking, but also a little ..." Daisy searched for the right word. "Not sinister, but rather ... oh bugger, I'm trying to find the right word. Brooding. He always has this troubled look about him. I like him; he tells it how it is and can't be bothered with games." She shot a glance over to her sister. "Probably why he and Aria didn't last. Anyway, he keeps himself to himself, as you know. Once upon a time, he would come have coffee, chat with some locals, but those days are gone. Shame." She studied Sunday. "And you really haven't seen him?"

Sunday shook her head. "I have met Luke Maslany, though."

Daisy's smile widened. "Oh, I love Luke. He's like a big teddy bear. I have such a crush on him."

"You should ask him out," Sunday told and Daisy laughed.

"Right ... He's a big-deal doctor, and I'm a coffee shop owner."

"So? Luke seems pretty down to earth to me, and there's nothing wrong with owning a coffeehouse. You're an entrepreneur. This place is wonderful. I'm sure I wouldn't feel so welcome anyplace else."

"You are sweet. But really, Luke is way out of my league."

Sunday looked at Daisy incredulously. Daisy was gorgeous, all soft curves and warmth. "No one is out of your league, honey."

Daisy rolled her eyes. "Sweet talker. How about you? Any boyfriends? Or girlfriends? I shouldn't presume."

Sunday grinned. "Dude, if I were into girls, I'd be hitting on you right now." They both laughed. "But no. No boyfriend. Not for a while now."

"There's a story there, isn't there?" Daisy said, reading Sunday's expression, and she nodded.

"Yeah. But for another time."

"Gotcha."

As Sunday walked back to her apartment, she glanced over at the diner, wondering if her erstwhile lover would turn up there again tonight. She had already decided she wouldn't be there. Last night had been wild, crazy, and exhilarating—and a one-off. She didn't need the complication, however much she craved that touch again.

Nope.

No way.

CHAPTER SIX

River crouched down to take his daughter in his arms. "Hello again, Pickle."

Berry, all dark curls and a huge smile, giggled. "I'm not a pickle, Daddy!"

"Yeah you are, big pickle. Hey, Linds." He stood, Berry in his arms, to greet his ex-lover, who smiled at him gratefully.

"Hey, River. Listen, I cannot tell you how grateful I am for this."

He waved her thanks away. "It's always a pleasure, don't be silly. Let's go grab some breakfast. I know airport food isn't that great, but I know somewhere we can go—if you have the time?"

Lindsey, a sweet, dark-haired woman, nodded at him, but there was something in her eyes that made him curious. "Of course."

As they ate breakfast in a diner an hour later, she told him. "Stage IV," she said simply, and River's heart broke.

"No. Oh God ... Linds."

"Just my luck, eh? Just the tiniest lump, barely able to feel it, but apparently, it's deep and spreading. Liver, lungs, brain."

"Jesus." River took her hand, and she squeezed his back. "Sweetheart ... listen, we can do something. Sloan Kettering or anyplace in any country that can treat you, we can do that."

Lindsey touched his face. "You are the sweetest man, River Giotto, but I'm afraid it's way past that now. It's okay, I've made my peace. It's just ..." She cut her eyes to Berry who was eating a huge stack of blueberry pancakes, a look of great concentration on her face. "I hate the thought of leaving ..." She looked back at River with tears in her eyes. "And I know you didn't ask for any of this, for us, for her but ..."

"Lindsey, it would be my honor, my privilege, and my absolute responsibility. I hate that you feel you have to ask. Of course ... of course ..."

Lindsey's shoulders slumped and she let the tears fall then. "I cannot tell you how relieved I am. I was so scared that she would be left alone."

"Never. Never ever," River said with feeling and drew Lindsey into his arms, hugging her tightly. "We are a family. An unusual one, yes, but then I don't know what normal is. You have my word, Lindsey. Berry will want for nothing, especially love."

They talked for hours. Lindsey told him the doctors had given her a few weeks. "If I'm lucky. I need to go say my goodbyes to everyone, but I don't want to traumatize Berry. If I may ... I'd like us to be together at the end."

"Of course. Look, I could travel with you. Take care of Berry. Then we can all be together the whole time."

Lindsey looked at him in surprise. "You would do that?"

"Of course. I understand why you want to protect her from the worst but believe me, she'll figure it out later and wonder why you went away when you could have been together. Trust me, honey, we can do this."

Lindsey started to cry again. "You are a remarkable man, River Giotto."

LATER, when Lindsey and Berry were taking a nap, River called Carmen and explained the situation. "Can I ask you to pack me a suitcase and have it brought here? I don't want to waste a moment with them both."

"Of course ... oh, it's just so sad. Listen, don't worry about anything. And I'll ... get a room ready for Berry when you come back."

River closed his eyes. "Thank you, Carmen. I know this is a strange situation. I hate to say it, but I don't think we'll be away for long."

After he hung up, he glanced over at his ex-lover and their daughter sleeping. There was no question in his mind that he would go with them to say goodbye to Lindsey's loved ones. He would make sure they traveled in luxury and were spoiled rotten by everyone. He had no idea how they were going to tell the child that Mommy wouldn't be around for much longer. How the hell did you make a five-year-old understand?

His heart throbbed with pain and he stepped outside the hotel room to smoke a cigarette on the balcony. Man, he felt like life was just running away with him, as if he had no control. Work, family, his failing eyesight.

And his father's diaries and the woman who was transcribing them for him. Sunday Kemp. Even her name made his cock harden. He'd watched her leave his home a few times, known she'd sensed him there, seen her shy wave. He'd even heard her tell him to come talk to her.

If only she knew ...

But for now, he had to concentrate, and maybe being away from Colorado for a few weeks would help clear his head. Maybe she would have finished transcribing his father's journals by then, found out about the horror of his family history, and would have left by the time he got back with Berry.

Maybe he would be able to stop thinking about her.

Maybe ...

NEW YORK ...

ANGELINA MARSHALL ROLLED over and slipped out of bed. Brian Scanlan watched her with a critical eye as she shrugged into a silk robe and headed for the shower. "You've lost more weight."

Angelina ignored him. It was true, she had lost weight, but she didn't see it as a negative. She could fit into every high-end designer sample and looked good doing it. Her high cheekbones were perhaps more prominent that she'd like, and the constant battle with the gray pallor of her skin was a nuisance, but otherwise, she knew she was a beautiful woman.

If she wasn't, then how was it that Brian kept bedding her? And the rest of them. Angelina didn't particularly enjoy sex; she just enjoyed the power it gave her over men.

"So?" She went to the table where six lines of fine white powder lay scratched out on the glass. She snorted two lines then nodded at them. "It's good. Enjoy."

Scanlan was already getting dressed. "Not my scene, but thanks."

Angelina smirked. "Since when? You're the biggest cokehead I know."

"Not anymore. I need a clear head."

"Ah. Is this the missing journalist skank?"

She didn't notice his eyes turned from gray to ice white. "She's not a skank. But yes, I have to keep my concentration if I'm going to find her."

Angelina sat back on the couch, crossing her legs and letting her robe fall open. "Surely her leaving town was a clear message. She's not interested. And why on earth would you still pursue after you tried to kill her?"

"I did not try to kill Marley," Brain hissed. "That was an error."

"You shot her in the gut, didn't you? Some mistake."

She barely had time to react before his hand was around her throat. "Firstly, I didn't shoot anyone. My hands are clean. Secondly, Marley wasn't the intended target and the man responsible has been dealt with. Thirdly, you keep your whore mouth shut or maybe something bad will happen to you."

Angelina wasn't frightened. In fact, his roughness turned her on and she looked at him with new respect. "Fine."

He released her and went back to getting dressed. Angelina licked her lips. "Why don't you forget getting dressed and come fuck me again?"

Scanlan stopped, considering. "Get over here," he said finally, and she obeyed him. He pushed her down onto the bed, unzipping his fly, not bothering to take any other clothes off. "Suck me," he ordered, and she obliged, taking him into her mouth and drawing on him, teasing his tip with her tongue. She smiled when she heard his groan, but then as she heard him call out another woman's name—Marley! Marley!—her anger erupted and she bit down ... hard.

With a scream, he cuffed her hard, sending her sprawling to the floor, her jaw on fire. "Fucking bitch!" He kicked her hard in the stomach, then, grabbing his jacket, he tucked his wounded cock back into his pants and stormed out.

Angelina rolled onto her back and smiled to herself. The

bruised jaw was worth it. Firing up that psycho Scanlan was more exhilarating than any sex. She'd met him a few years back and recognized the same narcissistic tendencies in him that she relished in herself. She loved the violence in him—it inspired her own bloodlust. When he'd had his object of affection shot, Angelina had laughed. Yeah, so maybe he hadn't meant to kill Marley Locke, but Angelina had been on the end of Marley's sharp intelligence once too often and she had crowed at the thought of the young woman—the way-too-beautiful for Angelina's tastes young woman—brought low by an assassin's bullet. She'd even managed to bribe her way into Marley's room as she lay in a coma after the shooting. Staring down at her nemesis, she'd wondered why Scanlan was so obsessed with her.

But then, Angelina knew obsession. Her stepson, only a few years younger than herself, was hers. River. Beautiful, vulnerable, brilliant River. Angelina had deliberately pursued Ludo in order to get to his son, managing to seduce the old man just so she could get close to the boy. But River had had more about him than she'd realized. Behind those astonishing green eyes was a man who knew what he wanted—and he'd seen right through Angelina. When she'd made her move, after Ludo's death, River had rejected her outright, his loathing for her a raging, angry thing.

No matter. In time, he would be hers. It had been a couple of years now and news from Colorado had traveled to Manhattan. River was losing his sight, or at least partially. She knew him enough to know it would kill him to be unable to paint.

Maybe it was time his loving stepmother paid him a visit to comfort him in his hour of need. Angelina laughed to herself. Yes.

Maybe it was time.

CHAPTER SEVEN

pril, Colorado …

AS FAR AS Sunday was concerned, the past two months, working on the diaries, making friends, hanging with the friendly folk of Rockford, had been some of the happiest of her life. Every day she would get up early, go share a breakfast coffee with Daisy or Cleo or sometimes both, then drive up to the Giotto place—even she called it The Castle now.

Carmen had told her that River had been called away for a few weeks and that when he returned, Berry would be with him permanently. In the second week of April, Carmen told her that they would be back the following week. "I have to get a room ready for Berry," she told Sunday. "I don't suppose you'd be able to help me pick out some things, would you?"

"Of course, I'd love to." Sunday was touched. She and Carmen had grown close over the past months and the fact that she trusted Sunday with such an important job meant the world to her.

They drove into Montrose and found a place to buy paint and art for the walls of the room. Sunday asked Carmen what Berry was like, what things she liked to do, and, finding she was a bookworm, ("just like her dad"), Sunday suggested they make her a little reading den in one corner of the room. "We can add string lights and pillows and make it a little escape place for her."

"I love that idea," Carmen enthused and laughed. "I kind of wish I had one myself."

"I swear, I'll never grow out of wanting a reading nook," Sunday chuckled. "Speaking of books, let's find some bookshelves for her."

They had a wonderful day shopping together, enjoying a lunchtime meal, then driving back, chattering away.

They spent the week preparing Berry's room, setting it up, and on the day before River and Berry came home, Sunday made sure everything was in place. She worked until after midnight and decided to sleep on the couch in her office instead of driving home. She could barely open her eyes by the time she was satisfied everything was ready.

She stripped down to her underwear and pulled a comforter over her. She was so exhausted, she fell asleep immediately and was only half aware when she felt someone slide their arms under her neck and knees and pick her up. She felt the cool of the night air, then, as she was gently placed on a bed and a warm blanket was pulled up over her, she mumbled some thanks and was asleep again.

IN THE MORNING, she woke and realized she was in a room she had never seen before. The bed was huge, dressed in clean white sheets and a navy-blue comforter. A robe lay across the end of the bed, and for a moment, she wondered if she was about to see someone come out of the en-suite bathroom.

But the room was quiet. She slipped the robe on and went to splash water on her face. There was a brand-new toothbrush and toiletries on the side and she quickly showered, shoving her underwear into the pocket of the robe. After brushing her teeth, she padded down towards the kitchen. She heard Carmen's voice, then a child laughing. Shyly, she poked her head around the door. Carmen saw her. "Hello, sleepyhead. River said you were out for the count."

River had moved her to the bed? She'd never even laid eyes on him, yet he'd been so gentle with her, so caring. She smiled at the little girl at the breakfast counter. "Hello. You must be Berry."

"I am, hello. You are Sunday?"

Sunday grinned. Carmen had told her Berry was precocious. "I am. It's very nice to meet you."

"Nice to meet you too," Berry said formally and got down from her chair. To Sunday's surprise, the little girl held up her arms, wanting Sunday to pick her up. Sunday glanced at a beaming Carmen, who nodded encouragingly. Sunday bent and swung the little girl into her arms. Berry immediately planted a huge kiss on Sunday's cheek. "Thank you for my book den. Auntie Carmen said it was all your idea. I love it."

Sunday flushed. "Ah well, you're very welcome, but Auntie Carmen was just as involved. We both enjoyed making it for you."

She sat down and settled the little girl on her lap. Carmen pushed a mug of coffee over to her. Berry watched her, grinning. "Sunday is a pretty name. You have nice hair." She curled a lock of Sunday's brown hair around her little finger. "My mommy had nice hair too. We made it look extra-special for the casket. My mommy went to heaven."

Tears pricked Sunday's eyes. "I know, sweetheart. I'm so sorry."

"I was sad, but Daddy told me that Mommy will always be on my shoulder. Like an angel." She patted her shoulder. "So, when I am lonely, I can touch just here and Mommy will be holding my hand, even if I can't see her." Berry looked past Sunday's own shoulder and smiled. "Isn't that right, Daddy?"

"That's right, sweetheart."

Sunday felt a jolt of electricity as she turned and finally saw the man who had hired her all those months ago, knowing even before she saw him that that they had indeed already met.

She turned to look into the brilliant, beautiful green eyes of River Giotto—the man who had made love to her that wonderful, unbelievable night.

SHE WORKED HARD to keep her cool, even shaking his hand as if they hadn't been naked with each other. Somehow, she got through breakfast and when she went to retrieve her clothes, she somehow knew he would follow her.

As she bent down to grab her jeans, she felt his arms slide around her waist. For a second, she was tempted to shove him away, to be angry at him for not revealing who he was, but the second his lips pressed against her neck, she was lost. She turned in his arms and gazed up at him. God, he was beautiful. His eyes were tired, though, and full of sadness and she couldn't help but smooth the lines at the corner of his eyes.

"Hi," she whispered.

"Hello again," he said back and then his lips were against hers. The kiss went on and on until they had to break away to breathe.

"I'm sorry. I should have told you who I was that night."

She shook her head. "It's okay. It was a perfect night."

"For me, too. But I couldn't bring myself to come see you here. I don't know why. Perhaps it has something to do with my dad's journals. I tried to separate you from your work, I guess." He stroked the back of his fingers down her face. "I wanted you the moment I saw you, Sunday Kemp. You fit in here so well, I knew it must be fate. But then ... Berry and her mom."

"I'm so sorry about Lindsey. It must have been so hard for you."

"Worse for her, and Berry. But at least she got to go on her own terms, with her family around her." He looked exhausted and Sunday wrapped her arms around his head. He rested it on her shoulder. "When I came home last night and saw you asleep on this couch ..."

"Where did you sleep?"

"Here."

She made him look at her. "You should have stayed with me."

He smiled softly. "I didn't want to presume." He drew his hand down her side, making her shiver with pleasure. He pushed the robe from her shoulders, letting it drop to the floor. "You're so beautiful," he whispered and dropped to his knees, burying his face in her belly.

Sunday felt his tongue trace a circle around her navel and dip deep into it. His lips trailed down her belly, then his hands were parting her legs and his mouth found her sex. She gasped as his tongue lashed around her clit and moaned softly as his fingers kneaded the soft flesh of her inner thighs.

She stroked his dark curls as he pleasured her and when she was panting and coming, he stood and swept her onto the couch. He pulled a condom from the back of his jeans, making her giggle at his mischievous look. "So well prepared."

He kissed her as he hurriedly rolled the condom down his straining cock, then Sunday wrapped her legs around him as he entered her, his thick cock burying itself deep inside her.

Their eyes locked. "God, I want you so badly," he almost growled as they began to move together. "I haven't stopped thinking about you since that night."

Sunday smiled up at him. "Me either. Damn it, River Giotto ... what took you so long?"

He chuckled but then neither of them spoke as the intensity built between them and they could only gasp each other's names as they reached their climax.

Afterward, he helped her dress, stopping to kiss every few moments. River ran his hand through his hair and laughed a little self-consciously. "So," he said, "welcome to the business."

They both laughed. "I'm sure we've just broken every workplace law there is," Sunday said. Her body was still tingling from making love to this man, but she couldn't care less. He was so different from how she had imagined him, yet she could see the pain in his eyes.

She placed her hand on his cheek. "I know we don't know each other yet, but I want you to know. I'm in this. I'll help out however I'm able, especially with Berry, and I don't mean that I expect anything from you. I just want you to know you don't have to do this alone."

River smiled. "You really are very sweet, my darling. I admit, I'm just taking each day as it comes." He stroked her face. "And I'm looking forward to getting to know you, the right way. Again, I'm sorry I didn't tell you who I was that night in the diner. I just ... wanted you."

"Don't apologize for that," Sunday chuckled, slipping her T-shirt over her head. She tugged her long hair out, letting it fall in messy waves around her. River was looking at her with desire in his eyes.

"God, you're beautiful." He drew her into his arms again and his lips found hers. God, he was intoxicating, but eventually Sunday drew away.

"I think we should take this slow, River. Berry is going to need you. I'll be here, when you need me, or want me."

"I'll always want you," he grinned, but then he sighed. "But you're right. Berry is my priority and I would like you to continue to transcribe my father's journals, if you don't mind."

"Not at all. It's fascinating."

River half-smiled. "Getting to know my dad?"

"If it's not inappropriate to say, I'm half in love with your father. What a warm, kind man. No wonder you want to know what he wrote." She smiled a little shyly. "He adored you, River, but you probably know that. There was one part ... may I read it to you?"

River nodded and she could see the emotion in his face. She sat down at her desk and scanned to the part of the file she wanted.

"Even if we never have another child, it doesn't matter. River challenges us every day; his quiet genius even at such a young age is astonishing to me. I could not imagine loving another child as much as I love my son."

She stopped and looked at River. He was looking away from her, out of the window, and she realized he was struggling. "I'm sorry, River. I thought you'd like to know ..."

"Thank you." He said it quietly but the emotion was raw. "I needed to hear it."

He held out his hand and she took it and they walked back to the kitchen together. If Carmen wondered about their clasped hands, she didn't show it and the four of them sat and chatted for a while until they heard Luke calling from the front door. Berry hopped off her father's lap and went to greet her 'uncle.'

Luke grinned at them as he came in, Berry riding on his shoulders. "Hey, folks. Everyone's here."

Carmen pushed a mug of hot coffee to him and he thanked her. He eyed his best friend. "So, you met Sunday, finally?"

River and Sunday exchanged an amused glance. "You could say that."

SUNDAY WATCHED AS RIVER, Berry, Carmen, and Luke chatted. This was a family, the closest she'd seen for many years. And now she was part of it? How different her life was, even in this short a time.

She felt a wave of emotion and excused herself to go use the bathroom. She splashed more water on her face and peered at herself in the mirror. Her hair was a mess but her skin glowed, her eyes bright and excited. Excited. She hadn't felt that emotion since before Cory died. Her body felt electrified, sensual ... on fire.

Sunday combed her fingers through her messy hair, trying to tidy it, then returned to the kitchen. She saw that Carmen, Luke and Berry had gone outside into the little courtyard to make snow angels. River smiled at Sunday, kissing her temple. "Are you all right?"

She nodded. "Just trying to get my bearings. A lot changed fast."

"I know the feeling. Look, I don't want to freak you out, and there's a lot for us to sort through, but I'd like to try."

"Me too." She slid her arm around his waist and he hugged her to him.

"I'm sorry I kept my distance before. Even before Berry and her mom, there was ... I was having some problems. I wasn't dealing with them. I still don't know if ... well." He gave her a half-smile. "I'm going to try."

Sunday was curious, but she didn't want to intrude. He would tell her if he wanted to. "I know something I've been curious about," she said with a smile, "I would love to see some of your art. Luke, Daisy, Carmen, they've all been raving about it. I know I could have looked it up on the internet, but I held out."

River's eyes became hooded and closed off and she wondered what she'd said wrong. "Maybe another day?" His voice didn't betray anything wrong but she nodded.

"Another day is great," she said, squeezing his waist as if to say 'It's okay.'

River gazed down at her. "You get it." Almost a whisper.

"I do. We all have that thing, River. That thing we can't face. It's okay. It's only human. If you need me, I'm here."

He turned to face her. "And you? You should know I feel the same way."

"We need to get to know each other."

He nodded. "We have all the time in the world."

River had no idea that soon, his words would come back to haunt him.

CHAPTER EIGHT

During the next few weeks, Sunday and River managed to both take care of Berry and make time to get to know each other. They fell into an easy rhythm—during the day, Berry was the priority for River, while Sunday worked. Then, at suppertime, they would all gather to eat and talk, sometimes joined by Luke, and even Daisy on occasion. After Berry was in bed, River and Sunday would sit and chat, getting to know each other.

The only downside was that Sunday couldn't tell him the absolute truth about herself. The potted history she and the FBI had come up with didn't cover barely any questions he asked her and Sunday found herself slipping occasionally.

The night River asked her about the pain he had seen in her eyes was the night Sunday almost broke and told him the truth. Instead, she told him about an ex-lover who had died in a road accident. River was sympathetic, stroking her hair as she buried her face in his chest, pink-cheeked from lying. She hated lying to him, hated it.

The one thing Sunday was adamant on was that she would not stay over. They would make love, then Sunday would slip from River's bed, kiss him goodbye, and go home. They weren't hiding their relationship, as such, but Sunday told him that it was too soon for Berry to see them together.

She also had to figure out how she felt about the whole thing. Her body craved his touch constantly, but he still remained an enigma to her. If she was forced to hide her past, then River was choosing to keep things from her. Sunday couldn't blame him—she didn't have the right to demand he tell her anything, but she felt he was keeping something big from her, something he would only talk to Luke about. It left her feeling as if there were a chasm between them that might never be breached—and at the moment, she was okay with that.

SHE SPENT a lot of time with Berry, amazing herself at how easily she found being in the young girl's company. She had never aspired to be a mother, and she would never try to replace Lindsay, but she discovered a bond with Berry that surprised her. Berry, wiser than her years, loved reading and often asked Sunday to come play with her in the little book den they had built for her.

River told Sunday to tell him if Berry was a distraction, but Sunday loved spending time with her. Sometimes, when Berry was feeling the loss of her mother keenly, Sunday would hold the little girl as she cried, and rocked her to sleep.

RIVER CAME to Sunday's office one afternoon as she was working. She was so absorbed in the diaries that she jumped slightly when she felt his arms slide around her. "Good afternoon, beautiful."

She turned in her chair to smile at him. "Hey there. This is a nice surprise."

River usually worked in his studio all day and they never interrupted him while he was working. River kissed her cheek and sat down on the couch. "I've been thinking ... I should take you out on an official date."

Sunday put her pen down. "You don't have to. I'm not the wine and dine sort of girl."

"I'd like to." He smiled at her but she could see the turmoil in his face. She took his hands.

"River ... there's not a rulebook we have to follow. We can make up our own rules. Neither of us likes games, and forgive me for saying so, I don't think either of us is ready for ... a big commitment."

She slightly regretted her words when she saw a flash of pain in his eyes. "That's not to say I don't want you. Of course, I do. I'm just not ready for more than what we have now. And to be honest, we still don't know everything about each other. Or actually, much at all." She tapped one of his father's journals. "I feel I know more about your father than I do you."

River was chewing his bottom lip, listening to her and he nodded. "I don't share easily," he began slowly, "but I'm trying. Some things, I'm just not ready for. But I know that I want you, that you are the person I would like to try and form a relationship with. I suck at these things," he sat with a sudden laugh. "I really do. But, still, let me take you out. Even if it's just for a coffee down at Daisy's place."

"We might run into Aria."

"Aria's a big girl and our fling was just that—a fling."

Sunday considered and then nodded. "Okay, you're on. We'll have to get a sitter for Berry."

This time, his grin was triumphant. "I already asked Carmen."

"Sneaky."

"You bet. So ... later?"

Sunday's eyebrows shot up. "Today?"

River grinned and leaned over to kiss her. "I'm impetuous. And impatient."

She laughed, cupping his face in her hands. "Fine. Just let me do a couple more hours work."

"Nerd."

"Shut up." She grinned at him—when he was like this, fun-loving, teasing—she could hardly believe it was the same man who had avoided her for so many weeks.

WHEN HE'D GONE, his good mood had affected her, and Sunday did the one thing she'd sworn she would never do … she googled her old self. Marley Locke. The New York news sites were full of discussions on where she was, why she had left—a couple of wildly insulting rumors abounded, but Sunday had known that would happen—even down to the theories that she'd committed suicide.

To her dismay, she saw that Cory's family had been hounded by the press, eager for answers. The photograph of his mother, looking drained and distressed, made her stomach hurt. *I'm so sorry.*

She watched the video of her co-anchors discussing what had happened—they told the truth—they had no idea when, where, and why Marley had gone. Sunday stared at the picture they showed of her, neat and professional in a tailored suit, blonde hair perfectly coiffed. Who was that person? She had thought she had made her life exactly what she wanted it to be, but looking back, she knew she had been groomed into becoming that person.

She sat back and saw her reflection in the huge glass window —dark hair messy, eyes wide and full of optimism, and knew that she would never be able to go back, even if the threats to her life weren't there. "No more Marley. Not ever again." She spoke the words softly but knew they meant everything.

She smiled to herself later on when River came to find her. He looked nervous and she knew that he was second-guessing his decision to go out in public for the first time in months. She held his hand. "Come on, big guy," she murmured to him, kissing his mouth. "Let's do this."

The first person she saw as they entered Daisy's coffeehouse was (of course, Sunday thought) Aria. Her expression registered surprise at seeing River then, as he eyes dropped to their clasped hands, her expression hardened and she turned away. Sunday felt sorry for her but didn't say anything.

Daisy, in stark contrast, almost crowed with satisfaction when she saw them. "Well, it's about damn time."

She steered them to a private table near the window. "Usual?"

"Yes, please." Sunday beamed at her and River chuckled.

"And what's your usual? Some hideous concoction with pumpkin spice and coconut?"

Sunday grinned at him. "You guessed it. Bring River my usual, Daisy." She winked at her friend, who giggled.

"Coming right up."

River stroked Sunday's cheek, smiling. "How is it I feel I'm being ganged up on?"

"Because you are. That's the way it works." Sunday took his hand and wound her fingers through it, touched when he didn't pull away. "So that's one thing I've learned about you. You don't mind public displays of affection."

He laughed. "I've never thought about it but no, I don't. I get that from my parents. Italians, you see?"

"Such a stereotype."

He grinned. "Maybe, but it's true. Mom and Dad were very affectionate, to each other, to me. My grandparents too."

"You must miss them."

"Terribly. I always wished for a sibling but for some reason, they never got pregnant again." River's eyes were distant, remembering. "Has he talked about her much in his journal?"

"All the time." Sunday studied him. "You never read them?"

River shook his head. "My eyesight is ... problematic. The print is too small for me, hence asking you to transcribe them for me." He stopped talking but Sunday realized there was more to his words than he was saying.

"River? You know, you can talk to me about anything. Anything. It won't go any further. Is there something wrong? I mean ... with your eyes."

River looked at her with those startling green eyes of his and nodded. "I'm losing my colors. Something called cone-dystrophy."

Sunday was appalled. "Oh, River, I am sorry."

He nodded. "Yup. It's been a few months since I found out. Luke's been trying to track down any treatment he can, but yeah, eventually, the world will fade to black and white for me."

Sunday didn't know what to say. He was an artist, for chrissakes. "Damn, River ..."

"I know. Look, I've been wallowing in self-pity for long enough. Now there's a little person who needs me. Being with Berry and Lindsay made me realize that I'm still lucky. I could be losing my eyesight all together. I can still be an artist; I just have to adjust my expectations. My plan for life."

Sunday squeezed his hand. "It happens."

"What about you? Are you where you saw yourself five years ago?"

She felt her face burn. "No," she said truthfully, "but it turned out for the best." *I'm alive ... and then there's you ...*

"So how did it change for you? Was it just because your fiancé died?"

Sunday wanted to tell him everything but she knew she couldn't. Instead, she spoke around it. "That was the straw that broke the camel's back, but things were going south anyways. There was someone ..." She broke off. How the hell did she tell him this without giving herself away. "Let's just say, there was someone who wouldn't take no for an answer and it made my old life ... complicated."

"Asshole."

"Big asshole." Her throat closed. "I don't want to talk about that, not tonight. Tonight should be about happy things."

"Hey, hey." Daisy interrupted, carrying a tray. "Here is your new favorite beverage, Signore Giotto ..." She placed a huge drinking jar in front of him, a weirdly colored concoction that made Sunday snicker and River's eyes widen.

"What the actual hell?"

Daisy winked at Sunday. "You ordered it. Now drink."

River manfully picked up the drink and took a swig, the whipped cream on the top sticking to the tip of his nose. His grimace made Daisy and Sunday bust up laughing. "Oh dear God, now I know what Satan's underwear tastes like."

"How dare you?" Daisy was crying with laughter. "I'll have you know that was my finest work. Hazelnut mint orange with just a hint of toothpaste. Oh, and coffee, of course."

"Toothpaste?" River was laughing now and Sunday's breath caught in her throat—God, this man was gorgeous. Sexy, fun, tormented ... he was everything, and that smile ...

She watched him and Daisy tease each other. *God, I could fall for you so easily ...* Sunday felt a pang of sadness, a feeling that by being with River, she was betraying Cory's memory.

No. Shut that down. After everything, you deserve happiness. She felt someone watching her and glanced over to see

Aria watching her, an unreadable expression on her face. Sunday excused herself and went to the bathroom, waiting a beat. Sure enough, a moment later, Aria came into the bathroom. She didn't seem surprised to find Sunday waiting for her.

Aria leaned against the sinks next to Sunday and for a moment, neither of them spoke. Sunday waited. Aria sighed. "I guess you and River are together now."

"It's very early. Very early. And I don't want to make an enemy of you, Aria. Of anyone."

Aria nodded, chewing her bottom lip. "Me and River ... I always kid myself that we were suited but the truth is, we weren't. I'm sorry to say it but I think he's too damaged to really know love." She looked at Sunday, her expression soft. "And I'm not saying that to hurt you."

"I'd rather you were honest," Sunday said. "I can make up my own mind, but as I say, it's very early. River and I ... we don't know each other that well yet."

Aria nodded. "You don't have to listen to me. I won't be offended. Just know. It'll be like walking on an icy lake with him."

She left the bathroom, and Sunday felt a wave of confusion. Was she just being a bitch? The answer came back to her. No. She knew Aria was right. River was damaged; it didn't take a genius to work that out.

She went back out to see River drinking on his own, Daisy having gone back to work. A simple black coffee was in front of him now and Sunday smiled. "Are you scarred for life?"

"I might be."

As she sat down, he reached over and took her hand. "So ... now we're on an official date."

"Looks like." She smiled at him, trying to read the expression in his eyes. "River, listen, this doesn't have to be anything heavy. Let's just enjoy each other."

He reached out to stroke her cheek. "I want to know you."

"And you will. We just don't have to do it all in one night."

He nodded, and they chatted easily and lightly until after ten. Outside, he took her in his arms. "Come back to the house. Stay the night."

She shook her head. "It's not time for that. Think of Berry."

She couldn't be persuaded and instead they went back to her apartment.

River gazed at her then bent his head to kiss her. His mouth was soft against hers at first, then as the intensity grew between them, his lips crushed against hers. Breath mingling, they stripped each other, desperate to be skin on skin. They never made it to her bed, instead tumbling to the rug. Sunday rolled him onto his back and straddled him, stroking his cock until it was rock-hard and quivering against her belly. She slowly impaled herself onto it as River groaned, his hands caressing her breasts, sliding down her waist. Sunday tightened her thighs on his hips as she moved on top of him, taking him deeper with each movement.

God, this man was intoxicating, his intense green eyes never leaving hers, his strong hands holding her as if she was the most precious thing in the world.

He would be far too easy to fall in love with, and that was a problem. A big problem.

They made love tenderly, then with increasing animal desire, until they were clawing at each other, River flipping her onto her back and thrusting harder and harder until she was screaming his name and coming, her vision exploding with a million stars as she climaxed.

Afterward, breathless, they held each other until River looked at his watch, regret in his eyes. "I have to get back for Berry."

"I know." She kissed him and they got dressed. Again, he drew her into his arms.

"Just tell me that we'll move forward. That you'll stay over eventually."

"I will, I promise. I just think Berry will need a period of adjustment. She may seem fine, but if she thinks I'm trying to replace her mom ... I hate to think she'd be upset about us. We just have to be patient."

River smiled ruefully. "I was never very good at being patient."

Sunday chuckled. "Time to practice. We have all the time in the world."

CHAPTER NINE

But the next day, when Sunday drove up to the Castle, she felt the change in mood immediately. Walking into the kitchen, she saw Carmen alone, her face grim. "What's going on?"

"Angelina Marshall. She's suing River for custody of Berry."

"What the fuck?" Sunday was immediately angry. "How does she even know Berry exists?"

Carmen sighed and indicated Sunday should sit. "Apparently she knew even before River did. From what we can tell, she's been stalking every girlfriend that River had, even down to the one-night stands. That included Lindsay. River's never talked to his girlfriends about what Angelina did and so, apparently, Lindsay thought nothing of it when Angelina contacted her."

Carmen rubbed her face, looking tired. "She was playing the dutiful grandmother for years, without River's knowledge. When she found out Lindsay died ..."

"That bitch," Sunday hissed, her heart breaking for River.

Carmen nodded. "Of course, she played the selfless grandmother figure to Berry, so the child doesn't know that she's an evil succubus. River is beside himself."

"I should go find him."

"Please," Carmen patted her hand. "He's been in such a funk this morning. I can't reach him."

Sunday made her way slowly to River's studio—a room she had never been in—and hoped he wouldn't think she was intruding. She knocked. "Come in."

She slipped inside and was assailed by glorious color. Vast canvases with vibrant pinks, reds, green, golden yellows and deep, ocean blues. She gasped a little, taken aback by the beauty of them. "Oh, River ..."

He was sitting, gazing out of the window and when he looked at her, she saw the raw pain in his face. She went to him and wrapped her arms around him. He buried his face in her neck, his arms tight around her. They said nothing for the longest time, just held each other. Sunday felt tears in her eyes. She couldn't comprehend what was going around River's head. To potentially lose his daughter to his abuser? It was unfathomable.

Eventually River pulled away. "Thank you for coming," he said in a low voice. "You seem to know instinctively that I needed you. That means a lot."

She stroked his face. "Tell me everything."

River squeezed his eyes shut. "Baby, as much as I want to ... I can't. What happened between Angelina and myself? It's too much. It's horrifying. All I want to do is keep Berry safe from that woman."

"But you have to face what she did to you sometime, River. Deal with it. Until you do, she'll always have this hold over you."

River shook his head. "No."

Sunday drew in a deep breath. "You know I'm with you, right? For whatever you need. But I'm not going to be an enabler. You need to deal with—"

"What would you know about it?" His outburst shocked her and she saw the depth of his agony. She touched his face.

"I can't know, River. But I've been in situations where I felt helpless. I'm just saying ... to be at your strongest, maybe it's time."

River looked away from her. "I can't." Barely a whisper.

"Jesus, River ... what did she do to you?"

But he said nothing. Eventually Sunday gave up, and standing, she touched his shoulder. "I'll leave you alone. Just know I'm here for whatever you need."

As she reached the door of his study, she heard him call her name. "I'm sorry I snapped at you, Sunday."

"It's okay. I'll see you later."

At suppertime, she joined Carmen and Berry in the kitchen. To her relief, Berry seemed unaffected by the somber mood of the house, climbing onto Sunday's lap and talking excitedly about her 'Nanna' coming to see her.

Sunday looked at Carmen. "Angelina's coming here?"

Carmen nodded. "River called her this afternoon, told her they had to talk. Angelina invited herself. She'll be here for the weekend."

Sunday felt a lurch of unease. A piece of her own New York history coming here, to her safe haven? Would Angelina recognize her? "The weekend? Damn it, I can't be here." She would make up some excuse to be away, not to risk her identity being found out. Damn it all to hell ... why now? When River needed her so badly?

Carmen shook her head. "It's okay. I doubt she'll stay long when she hears what River has to say." She cut her eyes to Berry and said no more. Sunday nodded, but sighed inwardly.

· · ·

She was still thinking about her last meeting with the Upper East Side charity maven. Sunday—or rather, Marley—had been looking into a pyramid scheme that had been operating in the highest of New York's society and had taken a call from Angelina, who invited her to interview her about a charity cotillion she was hosting.

The interview turned out to be little more than a guarded threat—shut your mouth about the pyramid scheme or I'll ruin your career. Sunday hadn't backed down and had run the piece anyway, albeit mentioning no names. Angelina had been furious and had done everything in her power to ruin Sunday's career ... and had failed.

In the end, though, the small scandal hadn't affected Angelina's machinations one iota. She still portrayed herself as a victim in every situation and traded on her fading good looks, not wanting to admit there were younger, more beautiful women in her circle, waiting to take her place.

Sunday had always regarded her as kind of pathetic but now that she knew the depths of her evil, she wished she had gone all in on her.

"Too late now." Sunday finished up her work and went home for the night.

At home, she dug out the burner phone and called Sam, telling him about the Angelina situation. "The problem is," she told him, "I want to be there for River and Berry, but the thought of her recognizing me ..."

"I understand. Look, yeah, it's a concern, but wasn't this a few years ago? Do you think she'd recognize you?"

Sunday stared at her reflection in the window and was suddenly unsure. She looked so different ... would Angelina know her? "I don't know."

"Maybe hiding away when you're obviously connected to the family would be more conspicuous," Sam said kindly. "And of course, we don't know that even if she identified you, it would make a difference. I say keep things as normal as possible."

"Sam?"

"Yes, Sunday?"

She hesitated for a moment. "Are you any closer to finding out who he is? The man who shot me and killed Cory?"

"No, sweetheart, I'm sorry. He'll obviously know by now that you've left your old life, but whoever he is, he's careful."

"I just wish I knew what he looked like or who he was. It's bad enough knowing someone wants to kill me, let alone not knowing who or why."

"Sometimes these things are so out of left field. You did the best thing, letting us move you away from New York."

"I never thought I would say this but yes. Weirdly, I feel like I have a life here now."

Sam chuckled. "Well, that's good news."

Sunday didn't tell him that she and River were in the beginnings of a relationship. For one thing, she didn't know what was going to happen now. She found she couldn't sleep and looked out of her window to see if Daisy's coffeehouse was still open.

A warm light glowed from within. Sunday threw her jacket over her sweats and went across. Daisy wasn't working, instead her barista, George, was on duty. Sunday didn't know him as well so she grabbed her coffee and went to find a seat.

The coffeehouse was almost empty at midnight. An elderly woman nodded politely at Sunday as she sat down. Sunday sipped her coffee, trying to calm her mind from its state of turmoil. The main thing was to support River and Berry through this crisis ... nothing else mattered.

She heard the bell jangle at the door and looked up to see a young man enter. He was tall, olive-skinned, and had a shock of dark curls. He smiled at her, his dark brown eyes merry, and then headed for the counter. Sunday looked away, not wanting to intrude, but then she heard him say hello. "Mind if I sit? I've been driving all day on my own and I could do with some company."

"Not at all."

She guessed he was around the same age as her, late twenties, and he had a joyful, fun-loving demeanor. He was a flirt, too, and he made her giggle as he introduced himself. "Tony Marchand," he said, shaking her hand. "All the way from Seattle, Washington."

"What brings you to our little town, Tony?"

"Snowboarding," he said. "I heard the ski place here was second to none so I thought I'd come see if they needed any help."

"It's the end of the season, almost."

Tony shrugged. "I know, but I thought I'd risk it. If not, I'll work anywhere. I just needed to get away."

"Bad breakup?" She guessed and he laughed, coloring a little.

"You saw right through me. Were you born here?"

She shook her head. "No, California. I moved here a few months back."

"Friendly town?"

Sunday nodded. "Very. I'm sure you won't have any trouble fitting in."

"Hey, did I hear River Giotto lives here? The artist? Man, his work ... it's sublime. When I was surfing last year, there was a guy with some of Giotto's work on his board. Man, I wanted that board."

Sunday smiled at him. "Yes, River lives here, but he's kind of reclusive."

"You know him?"

And how ... "I work for him."

"Damn, you're the person to know." He looked at her admiringly. "And, if it isn't creepy to say, you're really hot."

Sunday chuckled. "Thank you, that's sweet, but I'm kind of seeing someone."

"Just my luck."

"Where are you staying?"

"Out at the Cadillac Motel, on the highway. It's pretty clean, and cheap."

Sunday nodded. "Well, what I've learned is that this place is pretty much the hub of town. You need contacts, ask around in here."

"I will, thanks."

They spoke for a few more minutes, then Sunday said goodbye. She walked back over to her apartment and up the stairs. She almost shrieked with shock when a figure appeared out of the darkness.

River.

"God, you scared me," she said, half-laughing, half-pissed, but River didn't smile.

"I'm sorry. I just had to see you so I came into town. Who was the guy?"

Ah. "Some dude who's new in town. He just wanted some advice on jobs."

"And he asked you?"

Sunday was a little irked by River's tone. "Well, I suppose he asked whoever was around. That being me. Do you want to come in?"

She unlocked her door and River followed her in. He seemed on edge, and for the first time, Sunday wondered if he had taken something. She made him look at her. No. He wasn't high, he was just distressed. "River ... I was just talking to the guy. I even told him I wasn't available, if that makes you feel better."

River sat down on her couch and she sat by him. "Is it this thing with Angelina?"

He nodded. "I just ... I wanted to forget for a night. Carmel is back at the Castle. She said she'd stay with Berry tonight."

Sunday took his hand. "Come lie down with me."

He was still tense, even as she slowly undressed him. She pressed her lips to his, running her hand over his bare chest. "Touch me, River."

He slid his hands down her waist, his fingers moving to the zipper of her jeans. She stepped out of them and pulled him down onto the bed. She tangled her fingers in his dark curls as they kissed, then, as River moved his body on top of hers, she heard him whisper, "Are you mine?"

She nodded, meeting his gaze. "I am. I'm yours, River."

They took their time, which was unusual for them. Usually, an animal fire overtook their lovemaking, but tonight, it was more about discovery. In essence, she knew, they were still strangers, but tonight it seemed as if River was trying to give more of himself to her, even if he couldn't tell her about his past.

He trailed his fingers down her belly, stopping at the small scar at the side of her navel. "What's this?"

"You didn't see it before?" She played for time, knowing that if she lied, he'd know.

River waited, the look in his eyes telling her that this was an important moment. Sunday drew in a deep breath. "I was shot. Last year. When I told you my fiancé was hit by a car, that was a lie. He was shot too. He died."

River sat up. "Jesus. Jesus, Sunday ..."

Sunday sat up. "When I told you about the stalker ... it was him. Or someone he sent to kill us. The thing is ... there is more.

But if I trust you with the information, it could mean he finds me."

River ran his hand through his hair. "I won't let anyone hurt you, Sunday. Ever."

"And I won't let Angelina Marshall hurt you or take Berry. But, River, if we're going to trust each other, if this is going to work between us ... you have to tell me what she did to you."

He stared at her for a long time, then, almost imperceptibly, he nodded. "Okay. Okay ..."

And for the next two hours, River Giotto told her everything.

CHAPTER TEN

Then ...

RIVER SAT IN HIS ROOM, his headphones on, pretending to finish his term paper, but really sketching. He had no need to worry about the paper—he was at the top of his class for everything—even with a B-grade he would still finish miles ahead of everyone else.

Nerd problems, he grinned to himself, then jumped as he heard someone open his door. His heart sank.

Angelina, his father's new wife, stood in the doorway, backlit, her body showing through the flimsy robe she was wearing. River sat up and took his headphones off, winding the cord around them carefully. Why did he always feel like this with Angelina? He had hated her on sight, not just because she dared to assume the mantle of 'mother' to him, trying to replace his beloved ma. Worse though, were the times she was alone with him, and she made her intentions clear. Ludo might have been her target, but River was the prize she craved. Only a few years older than him, she had waited, through the courtship, then her marriage to his father, before making her move.

River had rebuffed her constantly but every time she was near, his heart pounded uncomfortably and he felt like cringing away from her.

"Where's Dad?" he asked now, keeping his tone even.

Angelina smiled, no warmth in her eyes. "Still at the party. I was tired so I took a cab home."

"Well, good night, then."

Ha. No such luck. Angelina came into the room and sat down by him. He leaned away from her but she cupped his cheek in her hand. "River. My darling River. Do you even realize how beautiful you are? Look at you."

She turned his head so that he faced the mirror. All he saw were his mother's green eyes, huge with tension and terror. He hated feeling this way. Would a man really be this terrified? No. He had to stand up to her. He got up off the bed but she was too quick for him. She darted to the door and locked it.

"No. Not this time, River."

He drew himself up to his full height, already six-foot-two at just sixteen. "I'll tell my father."

Angelina smiled, cat-like and merciless. "Oh, I don't think you will. All it would take for me is to say one word to him."

"He wouldn't believe you."

She laughed. "Sweetheart, I've been planting the seeds since before he married me. Have you seen the way your son looks at me, Ludo? Isn't his teenage crush adorable, Ludo?" She walked towards him. "Hasn't he grown strong, Ludo? What would a weak little woman like me do against all that brute strength ... Ludo."

River couldn't breathe, couldn't think. Her hand snaked down to cup his cock through his jeans and he staggered back, the edge of his bed slamming the back of his knees and then he was falling ...

CHAPTER ELEVEN

Tears were pouring down Sunday's face as River spoke, his voice a monotone. "It went on for a couple of years, until I could escape to college. But the damage had been done. I fucked my way through college, treating women like trash. I suppose it was my way of revenge. I wouldn't let anyone close. Luke, Carmen, they stuck around long after I told them to go to hell."

He rubbed his hands through his hair. "My dad ... he never knew. I hope he never knew. I just ... I wish I had asked him why. Why he married her, of all people. He must have known she was a ..." He broke off and laughed without humor. "I don't even know a word strong enough for what she is."

"That evil fucking piece of bottom-feeding scum," Sunday growled, incensed. She got up and paced around her flat. "That fucking bitch!" She screamed that last and River gave her a half-smile.

"Yeah, that'll do."

"I could kill her. I will fucking kill her ..." Sunday felt the same white-hot heat of the rage she had felt when Cory died coursing through her veins. "These people ... God. What gives them the right?"

"Nothing and no one. But they still do it."

Sunday sat down next to him and took his face in her hands. "She won't get away with this. I swear to you, right here, right now, River Giotto. She won't even get to be in the same room as you or Berry, I'll make sure of that."

River held her tightly. "I love your fire."

"No ... no, it's more than that." Sunday took a breath in. "River ... I know her. Or rather, I knew her."

River's smile faded. "What?"

Sunday sighed. "My name isn't Sunday Kemp. Well, at least, it didn't used to be. My name was Marley Locke, I was an investigative reporter, and then an anchor in New York. The part I told you about my stalker is true, and so the FBI gave me a new identity after he tried to kill me. But before that, a few years ago, I crossed swords with Angelina. She's a con artist and scammer of the highest order ... I embarrassed her in the press, but she still came back swinging."

Sunday sighed, waiting for River to get angry. He touched her face. "You had to leave everything behind."

She nodded. "Everything." She chuckled. "And the moment I met you, I didn't regret a thing. I'm more me here, with you, and Berry and Carmen, than I ever was in New York."

"Marley." He was looking at her as if he was trying to make the name fit. She kissed him softly.

"Sunday. Your Sunday. Always."

He leaned his forehead against hers. "I have trust issues, I always have. But with you ..."

"I'll never betray you, ever," she whispered and with a groan he crushed his lips against hers.

"Let's forget everything about for tonight, everything except you and me ..." He slid his hands under her T-shirt and with one swift move, pulled it over her head. He pulled down the lacy cup of her bra and took her nipple into his mouth. Sunday sighed with pleasure, dropping her lips to the top of his head.

River moved her to the floor and pushed her jeans down as his lips trailed down her belly. As his tongue found her clit, Sunday shivered, tangling her fingers in his dark curls. "Oh, River ... River ..."

"I'm going to fuck you all night long, pretty girl."

His tongue flicked and teased her until she was moaning for him to be inside her and, grinning, he launched his cock deep into her, pinning her hands above her head.

"You're so tight, Sunday, so much like velvet."

Sunday smiled up at him. "Only for you, baby."

River kissed her, his tender embrace contrasting to the pummeling his cock was giving her cunt. "You know I'm falling hard for you, right?"

"Ditto," she chuckled, then gasped as he quickened his pace, slamming his hips against hers. He made her come twice before whispering to her that she should roll onto her stomach.

"Yes?"

She nodded, then moaned as he eased into her ass. Anal was something she'd never done before, even with Cory, and she was astonished to find she loved it with River. He was gentle and caring and the strange new sensations shooting through her body made her scream his name.

They showered together, fucking against the cool tile, then tumbling, laughing, to the bathroom's cold, tiled floor.

It was almost dawn before they broke apart, panting for air, exhausted and sated. "As much as I want you," Sunday laughed, breathless, "I don't think my vagina can take anymore tonight."

"This morning," he corrected, snickering. "And I'm ashamed to say you've exhausted this old man."

"You are not old," she said, stroking his face. "You are the most devastatingly beautiful man I've ever met, inside and out. Yes, you have demons, but God, I'm crazy about you, River Giotto, and I swear. We are going to get our happy ever after."

River took her hand and kissed her fingers. "Was there a life before you?"

"I used to think there was. Now all I care about is us, our little family. Not that I'm presuming anything."

"Presume away. We are a family." River stroked his finger down her cheek. "I'm going to tell Berry about us. She knows we like each other—hell, anyone could guess that—and it wasn't as if Lindsay and I were sleeping together when we were traveling."

Sunday was surprised. "You weren't?"

River smiled. "No. I had already fallen for someone."

Sunday flushed with pleasure as he kissed her. Oh, how I love you ... But she didn't say it aloud. They had come great strides tonight, in trusting each other, in deciding their future.

For now, she only had one thing on her mind.

Stop Angelina Marshall.

CHAPTER TWELVE

New York

SUNDAY'S NEMESIS—RIVER'S abuser—was hosting a cocktail party at her Upper East Side party, but had long since abandoned her hosting duties, and snuck off to fuck Brian Scanlan upstairs. Not even snuck, Angelina thought now with a smirk as she sat on Scanlan's large cock and rode him.

Scanlan was a great fuck, big cock, and nasty in the sack, but more and more she craved her fix. River. Over twenty years, he had been her obsession, her personal shot of pure heroin. To Angelina, he was beautiful, almost magical, and the fact that she ruled him was all the power she needed.

And now she had an 'in.' The child. Of course, she didn't give a flying fuck about the child's welfare, but she'd been smart enough to groom the child's mother into a false sense of security, plying her with money and Angelina's version of love.

When she'd heard that Lindsay had passed on, and that River now was Berry's full-time career, she could have crowed with delight. Just as I planned. Now, with the custody lawsuit, River would have to see her.

Angelina could hardly wait. She was going to Colorado at the end of the week to 'discuss' Berry's living arrangements. Her spies in Rockford had told her that he was seeing someone, his secretary or something. She, Angelina, would soon chase the girl off. River belonged to her, and she would not tolerate another woman being on the scene.

Brain sighed and lifted her off his cock. Angelina blinked back into the moment. "What are you doing?"

"There's a lot of things I'll do," he said, getting up, "but being ignoring during fucking isn't one of them."

Angelina shrugged and rolled over to the nightstand, getting a cigarette out. "Don't pretend you care for me anymore than I care for you, Scanlan. Don't act all butt hurt when I know you're thinking about your blonde bimbo."

"Summa cum laude from Harvard is hardly bimbo material," Scanlan said, and there was an edge to his voice that made Angelina smile.

"Still trying to find her?"

"The world is a small place when you have as many resources as I do."

"And yet she still eludes you." Angelina was enjoying goading him. Scanlan always had a delicious air of violence around him, and Angelina wasn't impartial to playing it rough. "Tell me, what are you going to do to her when you find her?"

"Not that it's any of your business, but she will be persuaded that a life with me is her destiny."

Angelina rolled her eyes. "And, of course, an intelligent woman like Markey Locke will roll over and say 'Of course! You had my fiancé murdered yet I will still go along with what you say.' God, you're delusional."

Brian had gone very quiet as he dressed and now he turned to her, his eyes burning with rage. "You," he said, venom in his tone, "have no idea what real love is. Marley belongs to me ... she knows it and will eventually admit it to herself."

"Or?"

He smiled without humor. "Do I really need to answer that?"

Angelina walked over to him, smoothing her hands over his chest. "No, but I'd like to hear it. What will you do to her if she turns you down?"

Scanlan looked down at her. "I'll kill her, of course. What else would there be to do?"

AFTER SCANLAN HAD LEFT, and her party guests had dissipated, Angelina drew a bath and soaked in it for an hour or so. She thought about what Scanlan had said and knew she understood his drive. River was always present in her thoughts, in every one of her actions. She remembered the first time she had seen him, just fifteen. God, he was beautiful, dark shaggy curls, bright green eyes, and a tall, not-quite-mature physique. His father, Ludo, was a spectacular-looking man, to be sure, but he paled in comparison to his son. Angelina had made sure she lulled Ludo into a false sense of security, had made him propose to her, just so she could be around River.

And it had worked. The first time she'd seduced River, she hadn't shown how nervous she was. Threatening the boy into silence had been easier than expected. River adored his father and was terrified of disappointing him. It had made her plan so much easier. Two years, she had had unlimited access to the boy, then, when he'd escaped to college, she'd faked reasons to go see him.

It was only when he'd reached maturity that he'd begun to fight back. He hadn't turned up to meetings when she ordered, or he'd ignored her calls. She'd taken to drugging Ludo and driving to catch River unawares, but he'd always eluded her.

When Ludo had died, she'd known she had lost all hold on River. Ludo, somehow sensing that his new wife wasn't all she had said she was, had cut her out of the will entirely, leaving everything to River. Angelina, rich in her own right, hadn't cared about the money, but had been furious that now River had the means and the control to cut her out of his life entirely. And he'd wasted no time in doing so.

But now he would be forced to see her. She would be magnanimous in her dealings with him, offering joint custody, or even just asking for visitation rights. She had already reached out to a realtor in that small Hicksville town he lived in, to find a property. He wouldn't be able to cut her out of his life now, however hard he tried. It was so perfect, she could laugh.

Brian's words came back to her. If his obsession turned him down, he was prepared to kill her for it. Would she, Angelina, ever go that far?

Yes.

The answer came back to her straightaway. But what a goddamned waste it would be. But if anyone else got in her way —River's girlfriend, that annoying housekeeper, or Luke Maslany, who hated her almost as much as River did, then yes, she would dispatch any of them without a second thought.

But River ... She got out of the tub and dried herself, walking naked into her bedroom and pulling open the drawer of her nightstand. She took out the small photo album she kept there, amongst her vibrators, her dildos, her drugs—all of her favorite things—and opened it.

As always, her heart began to beat a little faster as she stared down at the photographs of River. She lay back on the bed and slid one hand into her bush, stroking her clit as she looked at his image. The thought of him inside her made her moan and she bit her bottom lip as her orgasm began to build. There would never be anyone for like River, she knew, and as she came, gasping and moaning, she vowed one thing.

You will be mine again, and this time, I'll never let you go ...

CHAPTER THIRTEEN

If River had thought Berry might be upset at about his and Sunday's relationship, he was very wrong. He told her over breakfast, before Sunday arrived for the day, and Berry shrugged.

"I know. You love Sunday."

River smiled. "Well, we're just at the start of whatever it is we're doing, so love is ..." He trailed off. Yeah, fuck it. Berry was right. He was in love with Sunday, had been from the beginning. "Yes, I do. But I haven't told her that yet, and I'd like her to hear it from me, okay?"

"Okay." Berry was busy pulling all the green loops out of her bowl of cereal—she swore they tasted nasty even though both River and Carmen couldn't discern the difference. "But you do. Momma said she could tell."

"She did?" River was surprised. He hadn't thought he'd said too much about Sunday to Lindsay. "You know, this doesn't mean I didn't care for your mommy."

"I know. You and Mommy loved each other but you weren't in love."

River grinned at his daughter. "How did you get so smart, kiddo?"

Berry grinned at him, her mouth full of cereal, and he laughed. Children had never played into his life plan but with Berry, he couldn't imagine being without her. Screw Angelina—she wasn't going to risk Berry's happiness for her own selfish means. He ruffled Berry's hair, so dark and curly like his.

"Sweetie ... you know Nanna wants to see you?"

Berry nodded. "Carmen said she was coming to see me."

River sighed inwardly but nodded. "She wants you to go live with her."

Berry put down her spoon and when she spoke, her voice was so small it broke River's heart. "Don't you want me to live with you, Daddy?"

"Of course I do! I'm just saying, Nanna is asking if, sometimes, you can go and stay with her. You don't have to. This is your home, Berry, here with me and Carmen and Sunday too, someday, I hope."

Berry smiled, a look of relief on her face. "But Nanna wants me to visit her?"

River nodded. He really wanted to scream that no, Nanna was just using her to get to him, but he didn't. Berry would not be exposed to Angelina's fucked-up plans if he had anything to do with it, but he had to give her the benefit of the doubt. Maybe she really did care for Berry—it was impossible for River to fathom that anybody wouldn't want the adorable little girl in their life.

"Hey, gorgeous people." Sunday walked into the kitchen and River's heart lifted. Just seeing her beautiful face was enough to make him happy these days. He kissed her on the mouth, just briefly, but she looked surprised, cutting her eyes to Berry.

River smiled. "Berry thinks we make a lovely couple. Don't you, Berry?"

Berry nodded eagerly and Sunday laughed, obviously relieved. "You two have talked?"

"Daddy is crazy for you," Berry said, then covered her mouth, thinking she had given away his secret. Sunday and River laughed, Sunday tickling the little girl and making her giggle.

"And I'm crazy about both of you." She pulled Berry onto her lap and smiled at River over her head. "You know I'll never try to replace your mommy though, right?"

Berry nodded, not fazed by the question at all. "I know."

River poured Sunday a cup of coffee, offering her some breakfast. She thanked him for the drink but shook her head. "I grabbed a Danish with Daisy this morning. I needed the sugar after last night."

River grinned and kissed her. "Damn right."

"You did a swear," Berry hissed at him, and he laughed.

"Sorry, Pooh. Listen, what say we go out for the day? We could go up the mountain, or maybe to Telluride for shopping?"

Sunday and Berry looked at each other and said, in unison, "Shopping."

River shook his head in mock sadness. "Women."

Sunday helped Berry get dressed. Brushing the little girl's curls, she wondered at how easily this little person had fit into their lives here and yet she herself had found a home here quickly too.

"Sunday?"

"Yes, sweetie?"

"Do you think you and Daddy will have a baby?"

Sunday felt tears prick her eyes. "Well, I don't know, honey."

"I'd like a brother or sister. No, sister. Boys are horrible."

Sunday chuckled. "They grow up into nice people though.

Like Daddy." Not all of them of are nice … she shook the thought away.

"I suppose."

"Listen, BerBer … your daddy and I are just beginning to figure all this out. There will be time to see if we want to have children together."

Berry suddenly clung to her neck and Sunday hugged her. "I miss Mommy."

"I know, sweetheart, I'm so sorry." She held her tightly. "I know she's watching over you, that she is with you all the time, even if you can't see her. That she loves you more and more every day."

Berry nodded, her little head bobbing against Sunday's chest. Sunday looked up to see River watching them. Their eyes met.

"I love you," he mouthed, his eyes intense, and Sunday smiled.

"I love you too." She knew the truth of it, and in that moment, it seemed more than right to speak it.

RIVER DROVE them into Telluride and they enjoyed a morning of walking around the stores, even the tacky tourist spots. Berry consumed far too much sugar and Sunday teased River about it. "You'll never get her to sleep now."

"Oh, ye of little faith. I'll just tell her one of my interminable stories about the history of painting. That'll do it."

Sunday pretended to agree. "Ah, yeah, that'll do it, all right."

River grinned and dipped his finger into the ice cream sundae in front of him. He smeared a glob of cream on her nose. Berry burst out laughing and Sunday tried to lick it off but couldn't reach with her tongue. "Silly Daddy," Berry said and with Sunday's help, drew a heart in syrup on River's cheek.

River looked at Sunday, his eyes dancing. "Do we let her get away with that?"

"Oh, no way," Sunday laughed and with Berry shrieking with laughter, they covered the little girl's face with syrup and sprinkles, making the other patrons laugh at them.

"Look at us." River was shaking his head, trying to clean himself and Berry up.

"We're walking works of art." Sunday lifted Berry into her arms. "I'll take her to the bathroom."

River wiped the rest of the syrup from his face as his phone chirped with a text message. His smile faded as he read it. "Goddamn it."

When Sunday came back from the bathroom, her smile faded when she saw his expression. "What is it?"

He cut his eyes at Berry and shook his head. In the car on the way back home, he waited until Berry had fallen asleep before he spoke. "Angelina is coming to town on Friday to talk."

"Christ."

"Yeah." He glanced at her. "Listen, I've been thinking. I don't want to risk her recognizing you. If you two have a beef then she'll think nothing about revealing where you are to the whole world and there's no way I'll allow that. Your life isn't up for negotiation in this."

"So what are you saying?"

"When Angelina's here, I'll deal with her. I'll allow visitation with Berry—supervised—but that's as far as I'm willing to go. For Berry's sake. But I want you out of the way. Don't come to the house; don't engage with her."

Sunday was silent for a time and River reached his hand over and took hers. "You know I'm right."

"I wanted to help you."

"I know, baby, but you still can. Research anything you can that we can use against her if it goes to court." He sighed. "I know what she wants, of course, but she's no going to get it."

"She wants you."

He nodded. "But I'm not available." He grinned ruefully. "Not that I ever was to her. Not since ... you know."

Sunday touched his face. "If she even tries anything ..."

"Oh, she will, but I'm a different person now. A man. A man who will shut that shit down the moment she starts."

"Don't be alone with her. Have Carmen or Luke there."

"If I can. Listen, will you stay tonight?"

Sunday nodded. "I will. Now that Berry knows about us, I will."

He lifted her hand and kissed it. "Thank you. Just knowing you have my back gives me great strength, baby. Angelina won't get her own way this time."

CHAPTER FOURTEEN

By the time Berry was fast asleep, Sunday and River were exhausted but happy to be together. River drew them a hot bath and they shared the tub together, stroking each other's skin, kissing. Sunday straddled him and he buried his face in her breasts, making her giggle.

"Pervert," she teased, and he laughed.

"When it comes to you, yes." His curls were sticking to his face and she swept them back with her fingers.

"God, you're handsome, Signore Giotto."

He grinned. "Listen, when this crap with Angelina is out of the way, I'd like us to take a vacation together. Italy. I own a place in Tuscany. Sun, nature, and plenty of room for Berry to play, while I take advantage of her stepmom in the olive groves."

"Ha ha, that's just poor parenting," she giggled, then sighed as he slipped his hand between her legs and began to rub. "She asked me if we thought about having children. I told it was way, way too early for that."

River considered. "Do you want kids?"

"The truth? I never even thought about it. With Cory, we had plans to travel the world, and to be honest, we didn't plan anything further than that. Looking back now, I don't know why. Weirdly, it felt like we were racing against time—and it turned out, we were."

River stopped rubbing her sex and instead held her. "I'm so sorry about Cory."

Sunday nodded. "The night he died … God, it was so quick, so final. He … the killer, I mean, said my name. I thought it was a fan; sometimes they used to hang out outside the studio to say hi or grab a selfie. I was smiling at him when he shot Cory. Smiling. God." She closed her eyes, remembering. "I just remember Cory's chest exploding, blood everywhere, in my eyes, and instead of screaming, I got mad. I went for the gun and he shot me. I still managed to scratch the crap out of him but it didn't do any good. They never found him."

River's arms tightened around her. "But you were hurt."

"The bullet missed my vital organs but I lost a lot of blood. And they couldn't get the bullet out; it's still lodged in my spine."

His fingers were immediately stroking the small of her back and she smiled at him. "So it's always fun times going through airport security."

"I hate the thought of you being hurt."

"We all have been hurt, whether it's physical or sexual or emotional. The main thing is—I got through it. You got through yours. And we're together. I love you, River."

"As I love you, baby. You are the first woman I have ever loved—romantically, I mean. And more than that, you are the first woman since my mom who I trust completely."

"Don't tell Carmen that." Sunday smiled at him but his eyes were serious.

"Carmen is Carmen. She's like my surrogate mother; sometimes I forget she isn't my mom. But you know what I mean. With my heart. I trust you with my heart."

Sunday felt tearful. "And I trust you with my life. If you need me, when Angelina is here, I'm there, baby. Fuck everything else. I'm with you."

THEY MADE love in the cooling water, then again in his bed. Afterward, he wrapped his arms around her and kissed her. "I'm looking forward to waking up with you."

"Me too."

River soon fell asleep but Sunday couldn't manage to drift off. She lay in his arms until she was sure he was fast asleep, then slipped out of bed. Maybe if she read a while, she'd be able to go to sleep.

The house was so quiet at night. Outside, the moon was full, and it cast a blue light throughout the house. The lake outside was as still as glass. Sunday went to her office and picked up one of Ludovico Giotto's diaries. Snapping on a small reading light, she pushed her glasses into her nose and began to read.

It wasn't until an hour later when she realized. Suddenly she knew why River had wanted his father's diaries transcribed. He wanted to know. He wanted to know if his father had known about Angelina's abuse of his son.

"Oh, God, please no ..." Sunday shook her head, scared at the weight of expectation she suddenly felt. If Ludo had known ...

Should she lie? If it came to it, was it better for River to believe his father was ignorant of it all, even if he wasn't?

"Fuck." She ran her hands over her eyes. What should she do?

She felt faintly nauseous and shoved the diary back onto the desk and shut off the lamp. She walked to the kitchen, grabbing a glass of ice water. She drained in then closed her eyes.

She felt him behind her and turned as he reached for her. His lips were against hers and she opened her mouth to speak but he shook his head. In the blue moonlight, he looked even more dangerously sexy and as he lifted her onto the counter and parted her legs, Sunday gave herself to him. He pushed her back and hitched her legs around him. His cock nudged at her and then buried itself deep into her. Sunday's back arched as River fucked her, both silent except for their gasps for breath.

She came, hard, and River muffled her cries with his mouth, his cock pumping thick, creamy cum deep inside her. As she panted, trying to catch her breath, he swept her into his arms and back to the bedroom, where they made love again.

Sunday stroked his face afterward as they recovered. "I love you so much," she whispered, and River nodded, his eyes on hers.

"You are my world now," he said simply, and kissed her again.

This time, Sunday had no trouble falling asleep in his arms.

OUTSIDE OF THE HOUSE, the man clicked off another few shots of the sleeping couple. The shots would be dark but he couldn't risk using his flash. Luckily for him, the bright moon illuminated the sleeping lovers and he managed to get shots of their faces.

Later, back at the motel, he sent them through to his client. A few minutes later, a bank transfer was issued in payment. A brief email told him, "Great job."

And that was that.

IN NEW YORK, Angelina Marshall started to laugh as she looked at the photographs, and she picked up her cell phone and called Scanlan. He wasn't pleased about being woken.

"What the fuck could you possibly want at this hour, Angelina?"

"Oh, I think you're going to want to speak to me much more nicely than that," she purred, victorious. "You're never going to guess who River Giotto's new paramour is ..."

15

CHAPTER FIFTEEN

A few days later and Sunday kissed River goodbye as she prepared to hunker down in her apartment for the next few days. "You promise if you need me, you'll call?"

"I swear to God. Christ, I'm going to miss you." He tangled her hair up in his fist and studied her. "Don't go falling for anyone else."

"Ha." She nuzzled her nose against his. "Don't let her get to you."

River smiled. "I won't."

SUNDAY HATED LEAVING HIM ALONE, knowing his abuser would show up there soon. She had packed a few of Ludo's diaries into a bag and planned to spend the next few days working. But, as she dumped her bag in her cold apartment, she felt the need to go out and distract herself from what was happening at the Castle.

She went over to Daisy's coffeehouse to see her friend. She was surprised to see her chatting to Tony, the young snowboarder, and Sunday quickly realized that her friend and the newcomer were casually dating.

Good. It saved any awkward flirting. "How are you doing? I'm sorry I haven't been around for a few days."

Daisy grinned at her. "Dude, it's all right. I know you and River are pretty loved up."

"You do?"

"Nothing stays secret here for long. I think it's wonderful and listen, even Aria doesn't seem too pissy about it."

Sunday rolled her eyes. "I'm glad. I could do without another enemy." Too late, she realized what she had said. "I mean, a jealous ex."

She smiled at Tony. "So, you two getting to know each other?"

"She's great, although I have trouble with the accent sometimes. She put in a good word with her dad for me up at the ski place, got me a job."

"I'm glad to hear it." She sipped her coffee then wondered why Tony was staring at her. "Something wrong?"

"Nah … it's just, you really remind me of someone."

Sunday's stomach gave a lurch of unease. "Oh?"

"You ever been on television?"

She forced a smile. "Nope."

"Huh."

Change the subject. "So what job have they got you doing up at the ski place?"

She didn't really listen to what he was saying, jolted by his possible recognition of her. It made her feel sick to her stomach, and she realized how much River was giving up to protect her. The least she could do was stay out of sight.

She finished her coffee and made her excuses but as she made her way to the door, it opened and Sunday's breath froze in her chest.

Angelina had arrived.

Angelina looked straight at her, but in her eyes, there was no recognition. Behind Angelina, a tall, handsome man with piercing blue eyes stood. "Excuse me, please," Sunday muttered as she moved past them and out of the door. "thank you," she said to the man, who smiled down at her.

"My pleasure."

She escaped across the street and locked her apartment door behind her. She hadn't realized that seeing a part of her past life would upset her so much, even without the obvious horror that Angelina had wreaked on River's life. Sunday felt anger, resentment, fear, and distress all at once and now she was glad she was alone so that she could cry and rant and get all of the pent-up pain out.

She cried herself out, then took a shower, a headache pounding around her temples. She decided she would not work today, but took a long nap, waking just to eat some quick pasta, then fell asleep again.

She woke, fuzzyheaded, when her cell phone buzzed. She smiled when she saw who was calling. "Hey, baby."

"Hey, pretty girl." River sounded calm. "I miss you."

"Me too, my darling." She hesitated. "Have you seen her?"

River sighed. "Yes … and I don't quite know what to make of her visit."

Sunday sat up. "How so?"

"Well, for one thing, she brought her fiancé. Bitch is getting married. Poor guy."

Sunday heard the amusement in River's voice and was glad that he hadn't been upset. "What did she say about Berry?"

"She wants visitation. I told her okay, but on certain conditions."

"Like?"

"Like she gets supervised visits. She doesn't relocate here. She doesn't expect me to be there, but someone will always come with Berry." He sighed. "I might have pushed it a little far when I told her to hand over her passport whenever she visits Berry."

Sunday snorted. "With Angelina, nothing is pushing it." She hesitated. "She saw me. I went to Daisy's to grab some coffee and she came in. She looked right at me and I swear, River, there was nothing. She has no idea."

River groaned. "Don't say things like that. We can't get complacent. Did you recognize the man with her?"

"Not at all. Who is he?"

"Some property guy from New York. If Angelina's marrying him, he must be rich. Brian Scanlan. Are you sure you don't know him?"

"Doesn't ring a bell. I'll do some research."

"That's my girl." He sighed. "Is it weird that I worry about you being alone there?"

"You shouldn't. I'm perfectly safe, baby. It's only for a couple of days, then I'll be back."

"Yeah, I know." River was quiet for a moment, and Sunday felt for him.

"Was it painful?"

"Yes. Just seeing her. I thought I'd lose it, tear her limb from limb, but I think that's why she brought the fiancé."

"What did you make of him?"

"Charming. Fake as hell. Good match."

Sunday laughed. "I love it when you're a bitch, Giotto. I love you."

"I love you too, sweetheart."

They talked for a little while longer then said good night. Sunday felt a pang of loneliness, listening to the quiet of the apartment. She went to the kitchen and grabbed some aspirin. *Maybe I slept too long.* Her eyes felt puffy from crying. She made some strong coffee and fired up her laptop, typing 'Brian Scanlan' into the search engine.

The top result was a professional website for Scanlan Properties, a high-end property firm in Manhattan. She clicked through the site until she got to the page about the owner. Brian Scanlan, forty-two, unmarried, was a self-made man, rich beyond belief thanks to a savvy business mind, handsome in a bland way. Ruthless in industry, he was a fixture of the Upper East Side society set.

"Then how come I've never heard of you?" Sunday muttered to herself. River was right. There was something hinky about this dude. She did a deep web search on his name but could only come up with the basic facts she already knew. "No one is this anonymous, especially someone as rich as you, Mr. Scanlan."

Her journalistic curiosity was piqued now. If he was in a relationship with a viper like Angelina, there had to be something in it for him. Okay, so Angelina was supposedly considered beautiful, but her vile nature precluded anyone with an ounce of humanity being with her, surely? Sunday sighed. Was she being unfair?

No. She hated Angelina with the fury of a thousand suns and anyone involved with her had to be bad. "If you mess with my man, Scanlan, you are dead meat." Like she could do anything about it. Scanlan, the little she'd seen of him, was a big guy.

She shut down her computer and went to bed, making sure the door to the apartment was locked. River's warning had made her nervous after all.

. . .

It was dark when she opened her eyes and as they got used to the gloom, she heard someone breathing. No, no, she was just imagining it. She closed her eyes but then she heard the floorboard creak. She sat up. Her vision was weirdly blurry when she saw the figure come toward her ...

Why can't I move?

The intruder came closer and she could see his face had no features, his body was wiry and his hands ... dear God, his hands were knives and he drove them into her ...

Wake up.

Sunday sat up, panting for air. "Goddamn freaking nightmares." Hissing out the words made her feel better. Shit, was she really turning into such a pussy?

She glanced at the clock. A little after 1:00. She knew River would still be up. She called him.

"Hey, beautiful."

"Gorgeous man. I was just lying here and missing the touch of your hands."

River chuckled softly. He knew what she wanted. "Feeling horny, pretty girl?"

"Always for you. Do you have any clothes on?"

"Just my underwear."

"Take it off."

River laughed. "I will if you will."

"Oh, I'm taking everything off."

He groaned. "God, I wish I could be there."

"What would you do to me?"

"I'd kiss every part of you, starting with your lips, then your throat. I'd suck on each nipple until they were rock-hard and raw. Where is your hand, baby?"

"On my belly."

"Stroke it for me. Pretend your fingers are mine. I love stroking your belly; it's so soft. I love running my tongue around your bellybutton. Can you do that? With your finger, I mean, circle your navel and pretend I'm there, licking it, teasing it."

Sunday moaned softly, her eyes close. "Touch your cock for me, baby. Pretend my lips are closing around it, my tongue sweeping over your wide crest. You're hard, so hard, baby, and so, so big ..."

She heard his sharp intake of breath. "I'm going south, baby, down your belly, and now my tongue is on your clit ... God, you taste so good, Sunday ... my tongue is in you, going deep, deeper ..."

Sunday, her fingers stroking her clit, writhed on the bed. "I want you inside me; your cock is so hard, so hard ... fuck me, River, please ..."

"I'm in you. Take it all, baby, that's it ... that's it ..."

Sunday came, crying out his name as she stroked her clit and imagining his diamond-hard cock filling her. "God, River ... River ... I love you so much ..."

She heard his long groan of release. "Sunday ... forever... I love you ..."

After they caught their breath, they talked late into the night. "Only one more night away from each other, then we're home free."

"I can't wait. Good night, baby."

"Good night, my darling man."

AFTER THAT, Sunday had no nightmares. But when she woke in the morning, she found the first note shoved under her door and felt icy cold shock clutch her heart.

I found you, Marley.

16

CHAPTER SIXTEEN

"We have to relocate you."

Sunday closed her eyes. "No. Sam, no."

She heard his sigh on the other end of the burner phone. "Sunday, I can't make you do anything. But if your stalker has found you, your life is in danger."

"I can't leave, Sam. I have a life here, commitments ... someone I love. People I love."

"You had the same in New York."

With his words, she realized that no, this wasn't the same. "No. It wasn't the same in New York. I didn't realize it then but my life there ended when Cory died. I was clinging to nothing. Here ... my life really began."

"You know we can't guarantee to protect you. I mean, we'll work with local law enforcement to track this guy down, but staying there, you're a sitting target."

"I know. I'll get through this, Sam. I need to face him."

"Do you know how to use a gun?"

"No, but I can learn. My partner has one in his home."

"Have you told him about the note?"

"Not yet." Sunday felt guilty. "I wanted to talk to you first, before I dump this on him."

"He knows about you?"

"Yes. It's a serious relationship, Sam. It's River Giotto."

"Ah. Well, the man knows about security from what I hear."

Sunday didn't say anything. She could tell Sam was worried. "Look, maybe I should reveal myself, call this guy out. Tell him to come for me. Get this over with."

"And if he kills you?"

"If he kills me, he kills me. At least it will be over." Her voice broke, belying her strong words. "I cannot live like this anymore."

"Okay, sweetheart. Look, is there anyone new in town? A stranger to everyone?"

"A couple. One snowboarding dude, and a guy whose big in property in New York."

"Who's the last?"

"Brian Scanlan?"

"Ah, yes."

Sunday felt her heart lurch. "You've heard of him?"

"Not many people in NYC haven't. And no, he's not a person of interest. So, who's the other guy?"

She told him about Tony and he told her he'd make some inquiries. "For now, keep out of his way. Just in case. Can you stay at River's?"

She sighed. "I guess now that the secret is kind of out, yes. His ex-stepmother is Angelina Marshall. She's in town."

"That viper."

Sunday smiled gratefully. "Oh, what I'd give for her to be arrested for something. Anything."

"Yeah, she's a piece of work, all right."

For a second, Sunday contemplated telling Sam about

Angelina's sexual abuse of River ... but it wasn't her story to tell. "I'll go to River's house."

"Good. And for the love of God, take care of yourself. Keep this phone close. I call you."

"Thank you, Sam."

SHE CALLED River straight away and he made her promise to stay inside with the door locked. "I'm coming to get you. Pack all your stuff; you're moving in with me."

The feminist in her rankled, but the lover in her loved his masterful words and she told him. He didn't laugh. "I can't make jokes while your life is in danger, baby."

He was there in less than twenty minutes. She let him in and he pulled her into his arms. She realized he was trembling.

"I'm so angry, baby. I should never have let you be alone."

"I don't know how he found me." She leaned against him, feeling only relief that he was there. "But it's time to finish this, once and for all."

River let her go and studied her. "You think I'll let you use yourself as bait?"

"No, and that's not what I mean. I mean I'm done running. You are my life and my life is here in Rockford." She saw the admiration as well as the fear in his eyes. "Then we'll face it together."

River kissed her. "You bet we will."

BERRY RAN up to her and threw her little body into Sunday's arms. "Sunny!"

Sunday giggled and swung her around. "My new name?"

River was hiding a smile. "Tell Sunny why you want to call her that."

"Well," Berry began, "You're Sunday, but also like a mommy, so I figured I would call you Sunny."

Sunday was moved to tears and she cleared her throat before answering. "I love it, Berry, and I love you too."

Berry smiled in delight, burying her face in Sunday's neck. Sunday held her tightly. River watched them, a smile on his face. "Family," was all he said and she nodded.

River told her that Angelina would be coming by later to see Berry. Sunday nodded. "Well, I'll be there. I'm not hiding anymore. Fuck that."

River didn't look happy but he had to agree. "I'm arranging security around this place and, please, honey, until he's caught, don't go out on your own."

She told him what Sam said and he nodded. "Yeah, I wondered about that kid. You think it might be him?"

"That's the thing. I don't. I mean, he said he recognized me the other day, asked me if I had ever been on TV. He seems so guileless and Daisy likes him a lot. I hope, hope, hope it's nothing."

River nodded. "Maybe ... no."

"What?"

"We could ask Aria to keep an eye on him. For Daisy's sake, she'd do it, I'm sure."

Sunday was skeptical. "It's just ... can we trust her? She's not exactly the biggest fan of either of us."

"To protect Daisy, yes, she would. Say what you like about Aria and her prima donna ways, but she adores Daisy."

Sunday nodded. "Okay."

River stroked her hair. "Are you ready to face Angelina?"

Sunday smiled back at him. "I'll try not to rip the bitch's face off, if that's what you mean."

"I love your fire." He hesitated for a moment. "Say, no biggie, but did you …"

"I haven't gotten to that part of your father's diaries yet," she told him gently, and he shrugged sheepishly.

"I shouldn't even ask with everything that's going on. It just would help when dealing with her."

"Is she still being … whatever it is she thinks she's doing?"

"Not so much with the fiancé around, but when he steps out … yeah. She made it clear I could make this all go away if I were to … ugh. I can't even say the words."

Sunday put her arms around his neck. "Listen … while we're dealing with her, let's give her a taste of her own medicine. I'll make myself known, if she doesn't recognize me this time, and I'll tell her I'm here on a deep cover assignment. A historical case … a story about the sexual abuse of a child of a rich man … and the outing of an abuser. It won't be true … but it'll give her pause." She shook her head. "Every time I think about it, I want to kill her, and to think she had the nerve to want to be in Berry's life …"

"Hey, hey, breathe," River said, then chuckled. "I guess we both could kill for the other."

Sunday nodded. "I would die for you, River. And Berry."

River took a deep breath in. "I feel the same but neither of us is dying for anyone. This is our family now, and there's nothing I won't do to protect it. Nothing."

CHAPTER SEVENTEEN

They decide to give Angelina a little shock. Sunday would wait until Angelina was settled, talking to Berry and River before making herself known. "I cannot wait to see the look on that bitch's face."

River chuckled. "I love the mischief in you."

Sunday grinned at him. "Stop looking at me like that, or we'll be still fucking when they get here."

"Now I have a semi."

"Bat it down, player."

Sunday marveled at their ability to joke around in the face of what was about to happen, but she had learned that it was their way. Losing your ability to see color and you're an artist? Joke about it. Facing your abuser? Kid around. Stalked by a maniac? Act like you don't give a rat's ass.

But it was in their hands clasping, the touching of their bodies, the meeting of their gazes that everything was said. You are mine, and I will die to protect you. Sunday saw that in River's eyes now and hoped he could see it in hers.

. . .

Carmen came to find them. "Vampira's here."

Sunday snorted and she felt River relax slightly. "Who's Vampira?" Berry came into the room, and Carmel made a face.

"Vampira is Carmen's pet name for Angelina," River picked his daughter up. "Because she's not a nice person."

Sunday was surprised at River's honesty. "But you shouldn't tell Angelina that Carmen calls her that," she said hurriedly.

Berry shrugged. "Okay."

Sunday went to wait out of sight while Carmen took Berry back to her bedroom. The first time she heard Angelina's voice, she felt white-hot rage. How dare this woman keep intruding on River's life like this, after what she had done? She heard the voice of Brian Scanlan, greeting River politely. Who was this dude?

She waited until they sat, and then she heard River speak. "So, after our last discussion, I should let you know things have changed. I will be applying for full custody of Berry, and I will ask the judge to issue a lifelong restraining order against you. You will never see her again."

There was a stunned silence. "This is not what we discussed."

"No, but it's what I've decided, Angelina. There is no way I will let a pedophile have access to my child. Are you crazy?"

Unseen, Sunday made a victory salute with her hand. Go get her, baby. She heard Scanlan clear his throat. "I'm sorry, I don't know what he's talking about, Angelina."

I'm on. "What he's talking about, Mr. Scanlan," she said, coming into the room, "is that your fiancée, Ms. Marshall here, abused and raped River from when he was fifteen years old until he was eighteen. She not only sexually abused him, but verbally and emotionally made his life hell." She looked at Angelina, who was staring at her in hatred. "Hello, Angelina, how absolutely horrific to see you again."

Angelina's lip curled. "My God ... Marley Locke." She didn't seem surprised.

Brian Scanlan blinked. "I'm sorry, who is this woman?"

"My name now is Sunday Kemp, Mr. Scanlan, but before I was Marley Locke, a journalist and news anchor in New York. And Ms. Marshall and I have history. I've been working deep cover to get Mr. Giotto's story about you, Angelina, and believe me, the evidence is incontrovertible. We have written testimony from his father and some of the staff Ludo employed and we'll be handing it over to the authorities."

She squeezed River's shoulder, hoping he would know she was making this up. "You're finished, Angelina," she said, her voice like steel. "We've already handed the evidence over to the police. I expect you'll be arrested when you return to New York."

"You bitch," Angelina was shaking, clearly rattled. "You think you coming here, spreading your legs for my son ..."

"Not your son. Not ever your son." River stood now, his height imposing. Even Scanlan couldn't match it. River's rage was white-hot as he stepped towards Angelina, who skittered to her feet and backed off. "You raped me ... you really think I would ever, ever let you near my child? And don't paint yourself as a victim, although I know that's your favorite position. Our Lady of Perpetual Victimhood. You're scum, Angelina." He looked at Scanlan. "I don't know your deal but run. Get out. Get away from her. She will suck the life out of you."

"Angelina, I think we should go." Scanlan gripped Angelina's arm, but she ripped it away and lunged for Sunday. Sunday was ready for the attack and deftly side-stepped Angelina, kicking out the back of her knee and sending her sprawling on the floor.

Angelina scrambled to her feet and tried again but Sunday, who was ready for a fight, waved her on. "Bring it, bitch. River can't hit a woman but I sure as hell can. Give me the pleasure, Angelina."

"That won't be necessary, Ms. Kemp." Scanlan seemed rattled. He hoisted Angelina to her feet and nodded at River. "Forgive me, Mr. Giotto. I had no idea."

Angelina made a disgusted noise but Scanlan practically dragged her from the house. Angelina was still screaming as Scanlan pushed her into the car. Sunday and River watched them drive away and then looked at each other.

"Did that just happen?" River said incredulously and Sunday busted out laughing.

"It sure did, cowboy. You nailed her."

"You nailed her. God, that was so hot."

Sunday kissed him. "Come show me how hot."

"Ahem," said Carmen, a grin on her face, returning with Berry. "Children present."

She looked at River, who swept his daughter up into his arms. Berry kissed his cheek. Carmen put her hand on his arm. "You all right?"

"I am," he said. "I told her. I fought her. I feel … better."

Carmen and Sunday both grinned at him. Sunday had tears in her eyes. "Never been prouder."

"Why don't I make us all some lunch? Any preference?" Carmen asked, the grin on her face showing she knew what they would all say.

"Pizza."

"Pizza!"

Carmen chuckled. "Come on then."

River took Sunday's hand as they followed Carmen back to the kitchen. "Thank you, baby, for being there for me."

Sunday smiled up at him, her eyes full of love. "Any time, gorgeous man. Any time."

ANGELINA DIDN'T STOP SCREAMING at him the whole drive away

from River Giotto's place and finally, sick of her shrill voice, Scanlan cold-cocked her with a punch to the temple. Her head made a satisfying crack as it bounced off the side window and finally, she was silent.

Scanlan sighed with relief. He wanted to think about Marley, about how she hadn't a clue who he was, what he was to her life. How beautiful she looked. Her hair, back to its natural chocolate brown, her big dark eyes, that full, pink mouth …

He was surprised she hadn't looked more scared, that she had been so open about who she really was. If she had come here to start a new life … well … clearly, she was sleeping with River Giotto. No matter. Let her think she was happy.

Scanlan drove out into the mountains and parked at an overlook. He stared out at the snow-covered ground. What now? Angelina hadn't told him about her abuse of Giotto and he marveled at her stupidity in trying to go up against him. So, he had lost his 'in' with them … or had he? He looked at the unconscious woman in the seat next to him. Angelina knew his secret … but if he ended up dead now, he would be the first to be arrested. That didn't mean he couldn't threaten her if she attempted to break her silence … He would have to tread carefully.

All he cared about was getting Marley—Sunday—into his life and away from Giotto. Maybe if he promised Angelina she would get River back when he took Sunday away … of course, he would never let that happen. He would kill Giotto, frame Angelina, and leave her to the consequences while he began his life properly with the woman he loved.

He wasn't stupid enough to believe Sunday would fall for him straight away—she would be too busy grieving for her dead Italian bastard—but slowly, she would realize his death meant she would finally be where she belonged.

Scanlan had abandoned his first plan of taking her to his

upstate New York compound. No. He would have to take her out of the country, somewhere the FBI couldn't find them. He bought an island, a tiny, private place in the Leeward islands. Somewhere she had no chance of escaping him.

Somewhere, if it came to it, her murder would go unnoticed, her body undiscovered.

Angelina gave a groan and he waited until she opened her eyes and focused on him before he smiled at her. "Wakey, wakey, Angelina. I have some good news for you."

CHAPTER EIGHTEEN

Sunday ran her hands down River's body as they showered together the next morning. He grinned down at her, water dripping from his dark curls, water droplets in his long, thick eyelashes. Sunday kissed him. "I love you." Her words were simple, but she meant them with her whole heart.

It was strange. Despite the threat to her safety, there was a peace in her heart with this man. She truly belonged here, with him, and nothing was going to break that.

River drew her close. "Listen ... we talked about going away. Why don't we just go? Before Berry starts school again, before the summer and everyone is taking their vacation?"

She leaned into his solid, muscular body. "Let's do it."

"Italy?"

She loved the hope and the excitement in his eyes.

"I would love that, so much, baby. I want to see where you call home."

So, after a few days of organization, the three of them flew to Italy. River's villa was just outside Siena and they drove through the hills, Berry exclaimed excitedly at the lines of cypress trees and the secluded, rustic villas. River drove up a small hill to his own villa and as he glanced at Sunday to see her reaction, he saw that her eyes were full of tears. She smiled back at him. "It's so beautiful, darling."

He followed Sunday and Berry as they explored the villa, its white painted rooms, cool tiled floors, and comfortable furniture. "I have someone who does the housekeeping for me, and a gardener, but I love to come here and just be alone. Now I have a family to bring here." He smiled at Sunday and went to open the shutters on the windows of the main room, a large open-plan living space which opened out on one side onto a veranda overlooking the valley.

Berry exclaimed with excitement at the sight of the pool. "Hey, shall we all get changed and take a dip? I could do with a cooldown," River asked his daughter, who nodded eagerly. He raised his eyebrows at Sunday, who grinned.

"Let's do it."

River and Berry beat Sunday out to the pool and when she finally emerged, she saw the admiration in River's eyes as she walked down to the pool, her already caramel skin glowing in the white bikini.

"Wow," River said, and Sunday grinned at his obvious lust. She stepped into the water and swam over to him. Berry was sitting in an inflatable ring, singing to herself, and Sunday snickered mischievously as she surreptitiously cupped River's cock through his swim shorts.

He groaned as his cock reacted immediately and Sunday swam away from him, giggling. "You'll pay for that later, woman."

They played games with Berry in the pool, Sunday and her

ganging up against River until he complained, laughing. Later, Sunday and River cooked a simple meal of roast chicken and they all sat out on the veranda as dusk settled over the valley.

After Sunday had put a sleeping Berry to bed, she came back out to find River opening a bottle of wine for them. He offered her his hand and she took it, sitting on his lap, and he drew her close. They sat in companionable silence for a while, and Sunday saw him gazing out at the scenery, eyes slightly squinted, and knew what he was testing.

"Baby?"

He sighed, nodding. "Yes. The colors are different to how I remember them. It's like I've spilled water onto paint and the color saturation is faded. Damn it."

Sunday covered his eyes with her hand. "Close them," she ordered, and he obeyed. "Now, River Giotto, you know what, say, Hooker's Green looks like. See it in your mind."

She waited until he nodded. "Now open your eyes and look at that cypress tree at the edge of your property. See it with that hue you can see in your mind's eye. See it."

River concentrated and she could see he was struggling. "Baby, remember how you first learned to draw. See it now as how you've been taught it looks, but rather how your imagination sees it. Light and shade. See the hue."

She watched as his bright green eyes focused and unfocused as he tried to see it her way. "Any luck?"

There was a faint smile on his face. "Almost, and I can see where you're going. It'll take practice."

"Anything worth doing will. This is the reality: you have a condition for which there is no cure. So we'll have to learn to see the world differently. Your art will evolve, perhaps not in the way you had foreseen it, but it will evolve. It's part of you."

River was looking at her, his eyes intense, and he crushed his lips against hers as she finished speaking. "We," he said with feeling, "you said we will have to see the world differently. God, Sunday Kemp, have you any idea how much I love you?"

She clung to him. "Show me."

He lowered her down to the cool tile of the veranda, covering her body with his. He stroked the hair away from her face. "You look even more beautiful in a Tuscan sunset."

Sunday grinned at him. "Coming from anyone else, that would be cheesy, but from you ... I'll take it."

River chuckled. "Good." He kissed her lips then trailed his lips along her jawline and her throat as he unbuttoned her dress. She had decided against wearing a bra in the heat of the Tuscan summer and River sucked on her nipples until they were rock hard and Sunday felt an urgent wet heat between her legs.

"I want you inside," she whispered and he smiled at her.

"You want me inside?"

"Yes ..."

He reached in his back pocket but she shook her head. "No."

His eyebrows shot up. "Are you sure?"

"I want to feel you inside me." She studied his eyes. "Does it scare you?"

River's smile answered her question. "No. Not at all ... I've been thinking about it since Berry asked you the question."

"I know it's quick, but I feel like ... my body is aching to bear your child. I've never felt like this before, that it's right, it's time."

She didn't have to say anything else. River's lips were rough against hers as he kicked his jeans and underwear off, and as he gathered her to him, hitching her legs around his waist, he nodded. "I want this too, baby, so, so much."

His cock was ramrod hard as she helped guide him inside her and he pushed inside her slowly, wanting to remember this moment, finally, skin on skin as they began to make love.

Their gazes never wavered, their breathing synchronized as River's cock thrust deeper and deeper into her. Sunday's thighs gripped his waist, and she squeezed her vaginal muscles harder around his cock, making him groan.

His hands pinned hers the tile as his pace increased and by the time she came, she was almost weeping with pleasure, his body owning hers entirely. She felt his cock pump thick, creamy cum deep inside her as he buried his face in her neck, murmuring her name over and over.

Afterward, they lay in each other's arms, a light breeze blowing over their damp bodies. River's hand splayed on her belly, his lips against her shoulder. Sunday gazed out over the valley. "It's unbelievably perfect here." She grinned at him. "Let's just stay here."

"Done," he laughed, then sighed. "But seriously, as much as I love it here, we have to go back. Luke's there, Carmen, and Berry has school."

"I know, it's a pipedream." She sighed. "And I still have to face whoever is stalking me."

"I hate to admit it, but yes. We cannot have that hanging over our heads, especially with Berry."

Sunday chewed her lip. "You know, if it came down to it … I would never put you and Berry in danger. I couldn't bear that. Whatever this is, it's between me and the psycho nutjob who killed Cory. It's my fight."

"Our fight. 'We,' remember. Always 'we.'"

She kissed him. "Let's just enjoy this vacation."

CARRYING THEIR CLOTHES, they walked hand in hand to their bedroom, where they made love again and then fell asleep, wrapped in each other's arms.

At 3:00 a.m., in the blue moonlight of early morning, River slipped from the bed and put on his jeans. He padded through the silent house, checking in on his sleeping daughter as he did.

He stepped out into the cool night and drew in a lungful of breath. A movement caught the corner of his eye and he looked to see the dark-clothed man approaching him.

FBI Agent Sam Duarte nodded at River. "Mr. Giotto."

River gave a wan smile. "Sam, call me River, will you? You're here at all hours, protecting my family. I think it's right we know each other's first names."

Sam smiled, but then it faded. "Does she know?"

River shook his head. "No. She thinks we're here alone and I want it to stay that way. For these two weeks, is all I ask. Sunday's had too long being watched by this asshole, and, forgive me, by you. I want her to think she's free." He sighed. "Any news from Rockford?"

"We've looked into Scanlan and Merchant. Scanlan's a pretty big deal in New York—it would be hard for him, given his visibility, to orchestrate that kind of campaign without there being some weak link in his armor, someone who would give him away. Marchand ... he may look like a surfer dude, but he's hiding something. He's rich ... and we're talking could buy Bill Gates three times over rich."

"Tony?" River was astounded. "I'm assuming family money?"

"Some, but mostly he's a self-made man. Older than he looks, too, and here's the kicker. He says he's from the Pacific Northwest? He was born there but guess where he was for the last five years?"

"In New York," River said, his heart sinking. Sam nodded.

"You got it ... and there's more. His apartment? Three blocks from Marley's—sorry, Sunday's."

"Shit. Anything tying him to her?"

"Not that we've come up with yet. He's still in Rockford, still dating that sweet girl from the coffeehouse."

"God, Daisy ... Sam ..."

"It's okay. We have people looking out for the kid. Her sister, though, is a loose cannon. No one has seen her for a couple of days."

"Shit. But I have to tell you, Aria does that. She likes to play mind games, especially if she thinks she's not getting any attention."

"Noted. Your ex-step-monster is still in town with her paramour, but there's a rumor the engagement is off."

River frowned. "Then why are they still in town?"

"Scanlan apparently is in talks to buy the resort. Seems he likes the place."

River shook his head. "More fool him. You say he's broken things off with Angelina?"

"Apparently. Look, we've looked into the guy, and he appears clean. Are you sure they are the only two newcomers to town?"

"As far as I know. Daisy said she'd put the word around, find out if there are any others, but it's a resort town. Season is ending, but we still get a lot of hikers and climbers. It'll be impossible to vet everyone."

"Just let us know anyone who Sunday comes into contact with, or anyone acting suspiciously."

"I will ... and thank you, Sam. I cannot thank you enough."

Sam nodded. "Just take care of her, and don't worry. You're safe here."

RIVER WENT BACK INSIDE and to the bedroom. He took off his jeans and slid back into bed. Sunday murmured and snuggled up to him. River kissed the top of her head but couldn't get back to sleep, his dreams wracked by horrific nightmares lately. The thought of someone hurting Sunday, of taking her away from him, had been a worse pain than Angelina's treatment of him and he knew, that since meeting Sunday, he had become a different person. A man he hoped his beloved parents would have been proud of. He knew now that, being with Sunday, and them being parents to his daughter, he had found his true home. When Sunday had asked if they could live here, it had been on the tip of his tongue to say yes, but he knew they had to go back to Colorado to face and to beat her stalker.

He couldn't live with knowing that at any moment, she could be taken away from him. That was not acceptable. So he had called Sam Duarte and, between them, they'd figured out a plan to keep Sunday and Berry safe and happy.

For now ... that would have to satisfy him, but he knew, without a shadow of a doubt, that he would do anything—anything—to protect the woman he loved, even if it meant killing another person.

CHAPTER NINETEEN

Sunday knew that the last two weeks in the beauty of Tuscany would be a time she never, ever forgot. In every way, it had been perfect, and now that they were back in Colorado, she felt a new strength in her. This was her home, this was her family, and she would fight until her last breath to keep them.

A week after their return, Berry had started her new school and was loving it. River was back working in his studio, and Sunday was continuing her work on Ludo's diaries. As she worked one morning, she heard Carmen calling her and River.

"You have a visitor," she said in a low voice. "It's that man who came with Angelina. He says he wants to talk to both of you. I can ask him to leave, if you want."

River shook his head. "No, I want to hear what he's got to say."

Brian Scanlan shook both of their hands. "Mr. Giotto, Ms. Kemp, thank you for seeing me."

"What can we do for you, Mr. Scanlan?" River's voice was even but Sunday could feel the tension rolling off of him.

"I wanted to come see you, to tell you that I am deeply sorry for bringing Angelina here. I had no idea of your shared history, and I also wanted you to know that I have broken off our engagement."

"What you do with your life is none of our concern, Mr. Scanlan."

"Brian, please. And all I'm saying is, you shouldn't worry that she will be in town. I personally took her to the airport last night. It's just, I myself will be in town for the foreseeable future." He smiled. "I cannot resist a business opportunity and the resort here is remarkable but underrun. I hope to restore it."

Sunday was watching him. "Mr. Scanlan, may I ask you a question?"

"Of course."

"It's just … I was an investigative journalist in New York for a few years and yet I have never heard of you. How is that?"

Brian Scanlan smiled. "You would probably have heard of my father, Dimitri Lascus. Lascus Property?"

Sunday was surprised. "Of course … I met him on a few occasions. He's your father?"

Brian nodded. "You're wondering about the name? Truth is, I was born out of wedlock, and I had never met my father until a few years ago. He took me under his wing and I worked anonymously for him, undercover, so that I would not be treated as if I had only acquired my position by dint of nepotism. It was my idea, and I think he respected me more for it. A year ago, he returned and passed his business to me on one condition. I rename the business in my name. He felt I had earned it."

Sunday nodded, slightly taken aback by his honesty. She looked at River and saw he was less impressed with their visitor.

"So you've broken things off with Angelina?"

"I have. I can't believe I was taken in by her." He shook his head. "Maybe I was too focused on the business and was taken in by her beauty." His blue eyes were serious as he looked at

River. "I just didn't want to be tainted by association, is all. If the deal on the ski resort goes through, then I'll be spending some time here, and I didn't want to start off on a bad footing."

"Fine." River stood up and offered Scanlan his hand. "You made the right decision for yourself as well as us. She's a vicious, soul-sucking aberration of a human."

Scanlan half-smiled. "I guess that's just about the worst recommendation a person can have. I wish I had known at the beginning." He looked at Sunday and smiled at her. "We can't all have your luck, Mr. Giotto."

AFTER HE'D GONE, Sunday waited for River to say something but he seemed preoccupied. She went to him and he wrapped his arms around her. After a time, he mumbled something into her hair.

"I'm sorry, baby, I didn't get that."

He released her and looked down at her, his eyes troubled. "My dad's diaries ... I know what you told Angelina, but ..."

"I lied to her. I haven't read anything that would indicate that he knew about the abuse. In fact, he rarely talks about her at all. He talks about your mother, and you, and Luke, actually. He liked Luke a lot."

River's shoulders relaxed. "He did. You know what? I feel as if Luke and I have drifted apart, and a lot of that has had to do with my sight. He thinks I blame him because he can't do anything. I don't."

"Tell him that," Sunday said, glad of the change of subject. "We should get him to come over for dinner. Daisy too," she added and River grinned.

"Are you matchmaking? Because last I heard, Daisy was dating your surfer friend."

She wrinkled her nose. "Something about that guy ..."

"I'm surprised. You seemed to like him okay when you first met."

"Ha, ha, jealous boy." They both laughed, but Sunday shrugged. "I guess, given everything, I just don't trust him. He might be fine, innocent as the day is long, but he's a stranger to town and he arrived just before the note."

"So did Scanlan. What do you think of him?"

Sunday considered. "Obviously, points against him for being with the skank in the first place, and yes, I think it's a little weird he's suddenly interested in buying the ski resort, but I'm not a property developer. He seemed genuine just now."

"I thought so, too, except ..."

"Except?"

River shook his head. "I don't know. There's just something ..." He sighed. "It's probably just the fact he was with her. I don't have a reasonable head on when it comes to Angelina Marshall."

"Baby, that's understandable." She hugged him. "Anyway, let's change the subject. We've talked enough about Brian Scanlan and that woman."

BRIAN THREW his jacket over the chair, ignoring Angelina. She was smoking, her lunch left uneaten on the table. "Did you see them?"

"I did. They think you've gone back to New York."

"I might as well, rather than be stuck here in this damn motel room. You might have booked me a decent hotel."

"Where you could be recognized? Here, it's cash only and they leave you alone."

Angelina made a disgusted noise and Brian couldn't really blame her. The motel room was gross, the bedspread probably seething with bacteria. But it was the only way to keep her close and unseen. He had no intention of letting her go back to New York; she was too much of a loose cannon for that. Besides, while he was dangling the promise of River over her, she would do what he wanted.

"So," she said now, crushing her cigarette out. "You still panting for that little whore? What do you think will happen? Why on earth would anyone leave River Giotto for you?"

Brian smiled, not rising to the bait. "Really, Angelina, what makes you think I'm going to give her a choice in the matter?"

He met her gaze and was gratified to see her shiver. Yes, she got it. He was the one with all the power here. A lack of conscience would do that.

"And what will you do to her when she fights you?" Angelina looked hopeful and Scanlan decided to throw her a bone.

"Sunday will learn to do as I want, when I want, how I want, or her life will be ended in the most painful way you can imagine. Slowly. Intimately."

That got Angelina. She smiled, cat-like, and sidled over to him. "Tell me," she said huskily, rubbing her groin against him. "Describe how you'll kill her."

Brian smiled and for the next few minutes, as he described the death he had planned for Sunday, he fucked Angelina, coldly, clinically. Not that she cared. She was too turned on by his bloodlust.

"Tell me," she said, afterward, as they tidied themselves up, "why her? When did you see her? When did you decide you wanted her?"

Brian rolled his eyes. "Are you really interested? Why? When did you decide you were going to rape and abuse River Giotto?"

"On my wedding day," she smiled nastily. "He was—he is—so beautiful. Who wouldn't want him? Those eyes, those dark lashes, that body. His mouth. Christ, the first time I made him go down on me …"

"Made." Brian looked disgusted and Angelina laughed.

"You have the nerve to judge me when you've just finished describing what you're going to do to Sunday?"

He didn't answer her but waited and Angelina sighed. "So, come on. Why Mar—Sunday? Why her?"

For a moment, he hesitated. Did he really want to share that first sighting of Sunday, Marley, as she was then? That time in the university library?

He'd gone there to find someone to kill. Another girl to kill. That was his thing and his father had known it—and encouraged it. "Just make sure you're never found out."

That was the real reason his father would not give him his name. But Brian was never caught. He never raped his victims; that wasn't what he wanted from them. He just wanted to see them bleed.

But when he had seen Sunday, he knew he wanted more. He wanted her skin next to his, to see her mouth open in an ecstatic gasp as he made love to her; he wanted her to bend to his will in everything. He wanted to own her.

The fact was she had graduated only a few days after he'd first seen her and then she had disappeared. At that time, he hadn't had the resources to find her and had not wanted to ask his father for help. His father, even more twisted than he was, would have wanted to know why he hadn't simply killed the girl. He wouldn't have understood Brian's need to possess her.

So he had returned to his old ways until that one day when she had appeared as a reporter on his television. Then it had begun. She had been quickly promoted to anchor and then his campaign had begun. Flowers to the studio. Following her home. Interfering with her life in small, but subtle ways. The day he had seen her with that idiot Cory ... God, his rage had been all consuming. He had gone home to his apartment, not even bothering to switch on the light. The neighbors had made a complaint about the noise coming from his place. Fuck them. It had taken all his control to stop from killing her then.

Later, when he'd come into his money, he'd used it to keep track of her entire life. He had people break into her apartment, setting up cameras everywhere. There was nowhere she was safe from him. He'd hired someone to apply for a job as a runner at the news station so he would know her every movement. The runner had been the one to tell him when and where she would be that night that he'd sent his man to kill Cory.

When the man had called him to tell him that he had shot Sunday too, Brian had howled down the phone. He'd snuck into the hospital, knowing that if she died, that was it. He would have no reason to live.

He still remembered the night he'd managed to get into her room, telling the night nurse that he was her cousin. The first time he had touched her hand, stroked her face as she slept. She had nearly died, they'd told him, but she was hanging in there. He'd had a half hour with her before he'd heard voices in the hallway and had made his escape, but it had been enough to know she was going to live.

Over the next year, he had bided his time, watching her recovery. He had not been surprised that, during her time at home, she had become suspicious, paranoid, even, and when she'd found his cameras, he'd mourned the loss of the uninhibited view of her life. She'd returned to work nine months after the shooting and he'd, again, thought he had all the time in the world.

Until Marley Locke had disappeared forever. It still haunted him that the only reason he had found her was some random hookup with Angelina Marshall. To Brian, it was just another sign that he and Sunday would be together. Should be together.

And soon, they would be, living together as man and wife on his island in the Caribbean. She would bear his children and love him and them like no other woman could. She would be his entirely, giving him her body, her soul, her heart. She would never mention River Giotto or his daughter again, or any other man. She would belong solely to him and he would decide whether she woke up every day, whether she breathed in and out, and for how long.

And if she disagreed, he would make her suffer the torments of the damned before he killed her.

CHAPTER TWENTY

For a few weeks, Sunday could almost forget that her stalker had found her. Nothing seemed out of place or threatening and instead, her happiness increased every day as she, River, and Berry became closer as a family.

She and River were also excited that they had made the decision to have a child, but as yet, she hadn't fallen pregnant. She wasn't concerned; they had all the time in the world and their lovemaking got better every time as they learned about what the other liked to do and have done to them.

She was also becoming closer to Daisy and to Luke as they invited their friends to dine with them. Daisy's relationship with Tony had turned to friendship, she told them, but that was okay. Sunday noticed Daisy's red eyes on one occasion and asked her about it but Daisy told her that it wasn't Tony who had upset her, but Aria.

"We're drifting apart," Daisy told her, "and I don't know why. It isn't anything to do with you and I being friends, I'm sure, but she won't talk to me, not about anything that matters."

"I'm so sorry, Daisy." Sunday hugged her friend, wishing she could talk to Aria for her, but not wanting to interfere.

By chance, she got the opportunity later the same week. She and Carmen had driven to a grocery store in Telluride, and as Sunday approached the bakery aisle, she saw Aria staring sightlessly at the bread on sale. She touched her arm gently. "Aria?"

Aria turned, blinking and gave her a half-smile—which was unusual in itself. "Sunday. Hey."

"Are you okay?"

Aria gazed at her for a long moment then shook her head. "No. I'm not. I'm not."

And to Sunday's astonishment, Aria started to cry. Sunday put her arms around the other woman and held her tightly, feeling Aria hug her back. She left Aria cry herself out before offering her a tissue.

"Thanks," Aria wiped her eyes and blew her nose. "I'm sorry ... I didn't mean to do that. It's just ... Sunday, I can't talk to Daisy about this. It would kill her."

"What is it, sweetheart?" That was something Sunday had never thought she'd call Aria Fielding.

Aria shook her head. "I found out the other day ... I'm sick. It's so ridiculous, I felt fine until a couple of weeks ago and now ..." She looked at Sunday. "Stage IV." She said it simply, and Sunday felt a jolt.

"Oh no. Oh, Aria, I'm so sorry. So, so, sorry."

"Thank you. I don't deserve that from you; I haven't been the friendliest to you."

"It's never too late." Sunday cursed herself as soon as the words came out. "I mean ..."

Aria smiled. "It's okay, I know what you mean. And you're right. It's not too late."

Sunday took her hand. "But I think you need to tell Daisy. The shock for her ... it's better to know. I know what it's like to lose someone in a blink of an eye."

Aria nodded. "I know, word travels fast around here. I Googled you. Marley Locke. Sunday suits you better."

Sunday chuckled. "I feel more myself as Sunday, strangely. That life seems so distant to me. Look, I'll be there for you and Daisy through this. Whatever you need, whenever you need."

"Thank you, Sunday. I appreciate that. Very much."

Sunday left her with a promise to call her later and arranged to go see Daisy together. Carmen was waiting for her, and she was smiling. "You and River are so alike sometimes. You both collect strays."

"I was one of those strays," Sunday said with a chuckle. "Thus proving families are made, not born."

"Amen to that."

As they were walking out of the store, Sunday glanced across the street. She saw Brian Scanlan seated outside a coffee shop. He must have sensed her scrutiny as he looked up and raised his cup to her. Sunday gave him a half-smile. She didn't particularly like the man and hoped he would not come over.

"Let's go, Carmen." She looked away from Scanlan and got into the car.

Carmen got in, then froze. "Shoot, I forget the toothpaste. Give me five, Sunny."

Damn it. As Sunday waited, she saw Scanlan get up and walk over. She rolled down the window, sighing, then plastered a smile on her face. "Hello again."

"Always a pleasure to see you, Ms. Kemp."

"Any progress on the ski resort?"

Scanlan smiled. "The papers were signed this morning."

"Congratulations."

"Thank you." He had his hands on the door and he leaned in

closer. "You must come by sometime. I can give you the personal tour."

The skin on the back of her neck prickled unpleasantly. She was absolutely sure River wasn't included in that invitation. There was something skeevy about Scanlan, she realized, something that made her stomach clench with unease. "Skiing's not really my thing, but thank you."

"There are other pleasurable pastimes aside from skiing. I could introduce you to some of them."

His meaning was absolutely clear now and Sunday, with relief, saw Carmen emerge from the store. She nodded to Scanlan, who backed away. "Another time, Ms. Locke."

It wasn't until she had driven halfway back to Rockford that Sunday realized what he had called her.

Sunday was quiet all through dinner and later, when Berry was asleep, River went to find his lover. She was sitting in her office, reading another one of his father's diaries.

"Hey, pretty girl." He sat down beside her and hooked his arm around her shoulders. "Are you okay? You seem a little out of it."

Sunday leaned her head on his shoulder. "Just thinking about stuff. Life. I saw Aria today."

"You did? Strange, I didn't hear about any girl fights."

"Ha ha." She chuckled then sighed. "We actually talked. She has some stuff going on, and she needed a friend."

"Wow."

"Yeah."

He kissed her temple. "Making friends all over the state."

Sunday nodded but she didn't smile. "And I saw Brian Scanlan. I think our first impressions of him were right. He's a creep."

River's eyes narrowed and he studied her. "Did he come onto you?"

Sunday nodded and River had to quell the pang of jealousy inside him. "I shut it down quick. Ugh. Why do men do that? He knows we're together, so why on earth would he think I would respond to him in that way?"

River choked back a retort. It wasn't Sunday's fault. "Not all men, but you're a beautiful woman. Douchebag likes to try his luck."

"Douchebag is right. As if I'd go for anyone who had been with Ange—shit, baby, I didn't mean ..."

River had gotten up and was pacing the room. Sunday got up and reached for him, but he stepped away from her. Sunday's eyes filled with tears. "I didn't mean ... you weren't with her, River, she abused you. I misspoke. I'm sorry, I didn't mean you."

River drew in a deep breath. "But I was with her. We had sex."

"No. Rape is not sex, River. It's violence, sexual violence. Did you ever seek out intercourse with her?"

"Of course not."

"Well, then." She gave a shaky laugh. "What I meant was, Scanlan voluntarily fucked that spider. Please, River, don't push me away; you must know that's what I meant."

For a moment, River felt like running away. He didn't want to feel sullied or unworthy of Sunday's love, but he had to admit—it was at the back of his mind, always. There was some damage he hadn't yet come to terms with.

Eventually though, he could not bear to be estranged from Sunday. He opened his arms and she went into them, the relief clear on her face. "I love you," she said, "I want you and only you, for all time. You are my reason to live, River."

He pressed his lips to hers, her words a salve to his fractured mind, and he knew, to move forward, he would have to deal with how he felt about what Angelina had done to him.

THE IDEA CAME to him during the night and he woke Sunday up, apologizing. "I need to ask you something before I chicken out."

She rubbed her eyes sleepily and sat up. "What is it, baby?"

"What you told Angelina, about you going deep cover to get my story—what if that was the truth? What if you went back to the career you gave up? Journalism. Help me tell my story, Sunday. The statute of limitations on having her arrested is way past ... but we can still expose her."

Sunday stared at him for a long moment, then she smiled. "You got it, baby. Let's bring Angelina Marshall down."

CHAPTER TWENTY-ONE

Neither of them realized what it would take out of both of them to relive and to hear the horrors of Angelina's abuse. Often, Sunday would end up sobbing with anger, or River would feel like he couldn't face remembering, but together they made it through the worst of it. Sunday worked on the story, and River was stunned and thrilled by her love of her profession, seeing finally what she had given up.

He, in turn, upped his efforts to find her stalker and rid them of his menace. There had been a few incidents that caused them concern—silent phone calls, wreaths of dead flowers left at the gates of the property.

"It's just so ... prosaic," Sunday said after one of the incidents. "It seems ... the whole time in New York, he didn't do any of this. I mean, he sent flowers, but not dead ones, and he never, ever called me. Maybe it's not him. Maybe it's Angelina fucking with us?"

"She would be that petty," River agreed, "and, yes, she doesn't have the imagination to be original."

"She's reading The Stalker's Playbook," Sunday joked.

"Was that the movie with Jennifer Lawrence?"

Sunday giggled. "That's The Silver Linings Playbook. The one Angelina's using has no silver lining. Not for her, anyway." She high-fived a grinning River.

As well as returning to writing, Sunday's friendship with Aria was a source of great joy and sorrow. She supported both Aria and Daisy when Aria broke the news of her cancer to her devastated sister, and River told Aria he would cover her medical bills. "We'll find the best specialists, Ari," he told her, "we won't give up."

Aria's whole demeanor softened and she would often come to play with Berry and have dinner with them. When her doctors told her that her cancer had spread to only one location in her body, her kidney, Aria found some hope at last.

Sunday and River's relationship grew closer as they worked together on the story. Late one night, as they lay together after making love, River splayed his fingers out over her belly. "One day."

"One day," she agreed, smiling at him. "I'm not going to stress about it. It'll happen when it happens."

They began to get complacent. Sunday would often drive to pick up Berry from school and although River wanted her to take a security guard with her, she often refused. "I'm not being caged, Riv," she said determinedly. "He can drive in a car behind. But I need to channel my Britney Spears when I'm driving and no one should be forced to listen to that."

River chuckled. "Fine. But he's behind you."

"No problem."

Sunday knew not taking the bodyguard would be trying

their luck. The phone calls and flowers stopped coming and she hoped against hope that her stalker had finally given up.

She parked the car in front of the school and got out, nodding to the bodyguard in the car behind. She walked into the schoolyard expecting to see Berry waiting for her. There was no one there and, frowning, she walked into the school.

The hallways were silent and she began to walk quicker, towards Berry's classroom. She pushed her way in and stopped, her heart thudding.

Berry's teacher sat, her face pale, as Angelina held a gun to her head. Berry, her face-tearstained, was in the arms of Brian Scanlan, who smiled pleasantly at Sunday.

Sunday knew, immediately. God, how had she not seen it? "Please … if you want me to come with you, don't hurt them."

Brian smiled. "Darling, you seem to think you're in charge. Here's how it's going to work. You and the little one will come with me. When we're clear of Rockford, I will call Angelina and she will release this lovely lady here."

"No." Sunday shook her head. "You leave her and Berry here, and I'll come with you."

"Hmm." Brian put his head on one side. "Let's compromise. Angelina, shoot the teacher, would you?"

"No!" Sunday lunged for Angelina, knocking the gun from her hand. "Run," she screamed at the teacher, who ran. Brian calmly pulled out his gun and shot the running teacher in the back. She staggered but kept going until she collapsed through the door into the fresh air.

Angelina had her hands around Sunday's throat, squeezing, squeezing. Brian, holding a screaming Berry, slammed the gun down on Angelina's head and she collapsed on top of Sunday.

Sunday pushed her off and scrambled to her feet, gasping

for breath. Brian leveled the gun at her. "Just the three of us then."

"Please," Sunday begged him, "leave Berry here. I'll come with you ..."

"No. She's my insurance policy. Now, move."

Sunday had no choice but to move, her eyes on Berry. "At least let me hold her."

Brian shoved the screaming girl at Sunday, who cradled her in her arms. "It's okay, baby, it's okay."

He made them leave by the back entrance. Outside, they could already hear sirens. "Get in the car and get down. If they see us, I'll shoot the kid first."

They got into the back seat of his SUV and Sunday held Berry tightly, praying that the police would catch up to them, that the teacher wasn't seriously hurt and could alert her bodyguard.

As they drove out of town, she studied Brian from the back seat. "Was it you in New York? Cory?"

Brian smiled. "You have no idea how long I waited for you, Marley. No idea. I watched you eat, sleep, fuck, live for years. I know every inch of you. You were mine the moment I saw in you in that library at Harvard."

Sunday gave a little gasp. "That was you?" She gave a snort of derisive laughter. "You know you were known as the Library Creep? That's what we all called you."

A satisfying flash of anger came into his eyes. "No doubt some of the girls I killed also called me that. They weren't laughing when they died, I assure you."

Her blood ran cold. She had to get Berry away from this psycho. "What is it you want, Scanlan? To kill me?"

"Not unless I have to, Marley."

"My name is Sunday."

"Whatever." He gave a short mocking laugh. "Sunday

Scanlan sounds good to me."

"Is that what it will take for you to let Berry go? Me marrying you?"

"Among other things."

God. "Where are you taking us?"

"Somewhere we can talk. Somewhere you can show me what you're willing to do to save the little girl's life—and your own."

Sunday knew she would rather die than let him touch her. "You'd better drive to Vegas," she said, hoping her bravado would hold. "Because I'm not doing anything until you let Berry go."

"Then Vegas is where we're headed," he said calmly, calling her bluff. "Our wedding night will be spectacular." His eyes met hers in the rearview mirror. Sunday held his gaze for as long as she could before looking away and she hated that he laughed when she did. "Good girl. Now, shut the kid up. We have a long drive ahead of us."

CHAPTER TWENTY-TWO

River felt an icy calm settle on him as the police and his security team told him what had happened. "Where are they now?"

"Heading out of state, we think. We're checking CCTV and the police helicopter is trying to track them down. They can't have got far."

"I need to be involved," he said, "You have to let me come with you."

"Sir ..."

"It's my daughter and my ..." he got choked up. "My Sunday. My girls. If you don't let me come with you, I'll hire my own helicopter pilot."

Eventually he persuaded him to let him ride in the helicopter. An hour later, they got the news there had been a sighting along the I-70. "We think they're in a black SUV. He's driving very carefully, under the speed limit, trying not to be seen."

River tried not to let his panic show. He just cursed himself that he hadn't seen Scanlan for who he was. What kind of coincidence would lead both of their tormentors to join forces? Had Angelina known who Scanlan was when she came to Colorado? River would bet on it. Not that it had done her any good—she was now in custody, charged with abduction and assault with a deadly weapon.

Angelina was refusing to talk, however, but River suspected that would change when she was threatened with a life sentence. As he traveled with the police, he was frustrated that they didn't seem to be trying to stop the car, however.

"Mr. Giotto, it's a hostage situation. We can't risk him driving the car off the road or hurting one of them in an effort to escape. We know he's armed. Let's figure out where they are going. As soon as he runs out of gas, we'll have him."

It seemed hours before they told him. "We've located them. We think they're going to Vegas."

Sunday sat holding Berry, who had finally fallen asleep in her arms. Sunday felt belligerent, ignoring Scanlan when he tried to talk to her. He simply shrugged and they drove in silence for hours. She had heard the helicopters flying overhead and knew they were being tracked and it gave her hope. She ran through every situation where she could attack him, and had she been alone with him, she would have tried, but she could not risk Berry's life. The whole kidnapping seemed shoddily planned—had he been forced into rushing it by Angelina? And how? He could have just killed her. None of it made sense.

All that mattered now was making sure Berry was safe. She pressed her lips to the sleeping girl's forehead and knew that even if Berry was her own child, she could not love her more. "I won't let him hurt you, BerBer."

Scanlan met her gaze in the rearview mirror. "Do what I say

and the girl will be safe. The moment you say I do, Sunday, I'll let her go."

Sunday said nothing. She guessed why the police were hanging back but wondered how Scanlan would imagine they would let him get away with her. Maybe he was counting on her telling them she had gone with him voluntarily. He was insane.

Of course, he's insane, stupid, she told herself. For one thing, he waited for years. Insane and delusional. Capable of anything.

"Were you the one who shot Cory? Shot me?"

Scanlan shook his head. "No. He was only supposed to take Cory out of the equation."

Sunday's eyes filled with tears. "Bastard. Cory was a million times the man you are."

"You have yet to learn who I am," he said calmly. "When you do, you will understand."

"That you're delusional? I think I got that." She couldn't help snapping at him, but again, he maintained an icy calm.

"Sunday ... our life together will be a happy one. I can promise you that. You will work to make me happy, or I will end your life. It's that simple. When we are married, I will have us flown to our new home. At any point, if you disobey me, I will add a few more bullets to the one lodged in your spine."

Sunday was rocked by this. "How do you know about the bullet in my spine?"

"I was there, at the hospital. I held your hand."

For Sunday, the knowledge that he had been there while she was in a coma was too much to bear. He really had intruded on every part of her life. "Why me?" she whispered desperately. "I'm nothing special. Why me?"

"You are a goddess." Finally, he sounded angry, passionate. "You, Sunday, are everything. Everything."

Sunday wondered how he could make such pretty words

sound so terrifying. She met his gaze again and saw he madness in his blue eyes. Obsession.

Oh, God, River ... I don't think I'm going to make it ... I love you.

I love you.

HOURS LATER, they drove into Vegas. Sunday's eyes were scratchy from exhaustion and the silent tears she had shed. Berry was awake but scared into dead silence. She looked at Sunday with huge, terrified eyes and Sunday held her tightly.

The car stopped and Scanlan made them get out. The Little White Chapel. It was tacky beyond belief and had she been there with River, they would have been laughing and joking around.

But the gun pressed to her side was no laughing matter. She saw unmarked cars pull up and a fleet of police offers get out but Scanlan merely grinned at them and forced Sunday and Berry inside.

Inside, the receptionist stood up in alarm when she saw the gun. "Hello," Scanlan said in a friendly voice. "One marriage please. Right now."

They were hurried into the chapel, another couple looking annoyed to be shoved quickly away. They were less annoyed when they saw the gun, more terrified as Scanlan asked them, with mock politeness to be their witnesses. They both nodded, never taking their eyes off the gun. Scanlan told the clerk to hurry.

"We seem to have some unwanted company, so if we could make this quick?"

River burst into the room, followed by a bunch of cops who had obviously been trying to stop him. "I object," he snarled.

Scanlan laughed. "We haven't gotten to that bit yet, asshole."

He reached for Berry but Sunday was too quick for him. She stamped on his instep then shoved Berry as hard as she could at the nearest adult. "Go!"

Scanlan grabbed her, pressing the gun to her again as River, grabbing his daughter, passed her to a police officer and turned back to face Scanlan. The gun's muzzle was hard against Sunday's ribs—if it went off now, her heart would be shredded in a second. River's eyes never left the gun.

"Scanlan, it's over. Let her go."

Brian's lips were pressed to Sunday's temple. "Not a chance, Giotto. I kind of knew it would come to this, but you being here to see her die just makes it all the better."

Sunday wasn't about to die quietly. She struggled with him, ramming her elbow into the center of his body again and again. Every police weapon was trained at Scanlan, trying to get a clear shot—if she could just ...

With one last try, Sunday used her body weight to try and throw him off, bending double with the effort. Shots rang out, deafening her and she felt herself being propelled through the air. There was pain. The breath in her lungs was pushed out of her.

Then River's arms were around her and as she opened her eyes, she saw Scanlan falling and felt only relief. She laughed, mostly from shock, and gazed up at River. "Hey, baby."

River's eyes were almost crazed. "Sweetie, hang on, we've got you ... hang on ..."

Why was he telling her to hang on? She was safe; she was free. "River, I'm okay."

He shook his head and she saw the blood. "No, baby ..."

As the adrenaline seeped away, she began to feel the pain—a very familiar pain. Oh, damn it, damn it ... not again ... not this ... her chest hurt ...

River's voice began to sound as if it were coming from inside a tomb, or from the end of a very long tunnel. "Please, help us, she's been shot ... she's been shot ..."

The last thing she remembered was his beautiful green eyes, full of tears, and his voice, begging her to live.

CHAPTER TWENTY-THREE

"Mommy?"

Sunday thought she must be hearing voices. Her entire body was aching, her head throbbing with pain. And she knew she wasn't a mommy. Not yet. Maybe not ever.

"Mommy?"

She opened her eyes to see a gorgeous, dark-haired child with bright green eyes being held by the most beautiful man she had ever seen. "Am I dead?"

"No, baby, no." The beautiful man was choking back tears. "No, my darling, you're going to be okay."

"Mommy." The little girl reached out and Sunday held her arms out. He put the girl into them.

"Careful, Berry, don't hurt Mommy."

But I'm not her mommy. I wish I was, I wish, I wish ... But Sunday held Berry close, breathing in her comforting smell. "Hello, baby, baby, baby."

"I love you, Mommy." Berry's hot little breath on her cheek as she kissed her.

"I wish I was your mommy," Sunday began to cry, "I wish I was."

"You are my mommy," Berry said fervently. "I prayed and asked my Mommy Lindsay if she would mind if I had a new mommy. I said I would never forget her, I promised. Daddy said I could have two mommies if I wanted."

Sunday started to cry in earnest then. Red-eyed, River sat down on the edge of the bed. Sunday looked up at him. "What happened?"

"Scanlan got off a shot before they killed him. It hit your ribcage and bounced off but broke your rib. They were worried the broken rib had pierced your heart but you were lucky. We were lucky. God, Sunday, I love you so much ... I was so scared I lost you."

"Never," she said, "You'll never lose me."

He bent down and kissed her mouth. "This is us. This is our family."

"And we are unbreakable," she said fervently.

Berry looked at them. "Daddy, Mommy ... when are you going to get married?"

River grinned, looking at Sunday. "The minute Mommy says ..."

"Yes," Sunday finished for him and they laughed. "Hell, yes."

Berry looked delighted but also, she made a face. "You did a swear."

"So I did ... forgive me?"

Berry nodded and they laughed. River stroked Sunday's hair. "You have some other visitors. Carmen, Daisy, and Aria are outside."

"Well, bring them in! I'll need some maids of honor to go along with my flower girl, here."

. . .

Carmen, Daisy and Aria all hugged her gently, and Sunday found herself overwhelmed by the love of her friends. Her family.

River excused himself a little while later and came back an hour later. "Sweetheart, there are some people here who want to see you ... can I ask them to come in? You're not too tired, are you?"

She shook her head, curious to see who it was. Carmen, Daisy, and Aria were clearly in on the secret because they all grinned and made room next to her. River poked his head out of the door. "You can come in now."

The first person through the door took Sunday's breath away. Rae, her assistant from New York, gave a cry and threw herself at Sunday, who burst into tears, hugging her old friend back hard. Her old boss and some of the old team were next, and then, lastly, a visitor who Sunday—or Marley—had never expected to see again.

Patricia Wheeler, Cory's mother, stood in the doorway and they gazed at each other. For a moment, neither said anything. Then Patricia held out her hands and said simply, "Forgive me, darling. I should never have abandoned you."

As the two women hugged tightly, Sunday looked over Patricia's shoulder at her family, her extended family, and then at her love. River. "Thank you," she mouthed at him, "and I love you."

A month later, back in Colorado, their lives settling back down, Sunday went to find River. He was in his studio, painting, determined to work with his new reality. The colors in his eyes were fading fast now but he refused to get down about it.

She went to him, slipping her arms around him and feeling him kiss her forehead. "Hey, baby."

She looked up at him. "Hey, gorgeous. I finished them."

"My dad's diaries?"

She nodded and he took a deep breath in, waiting for her to tell him what she knew.

Sunday smiled up at him. "He didn't know anything, Riv. He knew nothing about her abusing you."

The relief was obvious. River's body sagged and he let out a long breath. "Thank God. Thank God."

"The cherry on top is ... he knew he'd made a mistake by marrying her. He was planning to divorce her; he'd already cut her out of the will, as you know. All he cared about was you."

River leaned his head on top of hers. "I'm glad he didn't know, for his sake and mine. It would have killed him."

"He loved you so much, River, and he was so proud of you. So, so proud of the man you had become."

"Thank you, baby. God ..." He picked her up and twirled her around and Sunday giggled. As he put her down, he crushed his lips against hers. "We should celebrate."

He was already unbuttoning her short as she smiled up at him. "Well, Berry is asleep ..."

"Then we shouldn't be too loud."

"Good luck with that," she laughed as he pushed her shirt from her shoulders and they began to make love long into the night.

THE END

SIGN UP TO RECEIVE FREE BOOKS

Sign Up to Receive Free E-Books and Audiobook Codes.

Would you like to read **The Unexpected Nanny, Dirty Little Virgin** and **other romance books** for **free**?

You can sign up to receive these free e-books and audiobooks by typing this link into your browser:

https://www.steamyromance.info/free-books-and-audiobooks-hot-and-steamy/

Or this one:

https://www.steamyromance.info/the-unexpected-nanny-free/

PREVIEW OF THE VIRGIN'S DANCE

An Older Man/Younger Woman Romance

By Michelle Love

Blurb

It took me by surprise, but now I can't stop thinking about him.
Pilot Scamo. World-famous photographer. Billionaire. Drop-dead gorgeous man. Broken man. He's nearly twice my age but I've never felt this connection before … I feel it everywhere, my heart, my head, my body. It's like electricity when he touches me, kisses me, When he makes passionate love to me. He's intoxicating and all I want now is to hold him, Protect him, love him. Will they let us be? We both have so much dark history, so many

people against us. I'll fight for you, Pilot, even if it costs me everything ... I'll fight for you...
This book is a full-length standalone novel with a guaranteed HEA, no cliffhanger and plenty of steam. Exclusive bonus content included.

In the cutthroat world of contemporary ballet, young principal dancer Boheme Dali is already a trailblazer. The first Indian American woman to become principal at a major New York ballet company, Boh hides the tragedy of her past as she works tirelessly to become prima ballerina and make her mark on the world.
What she doesn't expect is to fall in love. But when world-renowned photographer Pilot Scamo, heir to a vast fortune, comes into her life, she discovers a soulmate and a creative partner like no other.
A passionate, sensual affair begins as Boh and Pilot begin to work on a project which will bring them both plaudits and fame, but at the center of it all are two people, both traumatized and damaged, who discover something beautiful.
Soon enough though, dark forces swirl around the happy couple, and a serious of tragic and horrifying events threaten to destroy their happiness. Can Boh and Pilot's love survive everything working against them and can they find their happy ever after?

∽

New York City

September

She stood on the roof, looking down at the stream of diamonds and pearls, the headlights and taillights of the cars flowing through Manhattan's streets. She liked the way it moved like a flood of sparkles beneath her, like the theater lights flickered when she was dancing.

Her feet scuffed along the concrete wall that surrounded the roof. It had been so easy to get up here. She smiled. Normally heights would make her stomach knot up and her legs shake, but not tonight. No, tonight was a command performance, and she was ready. She stood en pointe, ready to begin as the music in her head began to play.

Glissade, jeté, pas de bourrée, brisé. Along the wall to the far corner of the building. She had chosen this particular building because of its significance to her. To him. She could have gone to the ballet company's own building in Tribeca, but no, this building was her choice for her final performance.

In this building, three floors below her, he was fucking his latest whore. She counted—this was his sixth since the divorce, since he'd left her with nothing. Fuck you, Kristof, just fuck you. She'd enjoyed posting the letter to the New York Times, detailing Kristof's ill-treatment of her, the drug-taking, the philandering. Fuck him and fuck that ballet company. She was the prima, she would always be the prima ...

She stood, en pointe, at the corner of the wall, and spread out her arms gracefully, her fingers perfectly placed, preparing for her *grand jeté*.

The big leap.

She smiled, bent her knees, and took off.

CHAPTER ONE

New York City

One year later

Pilot Scamo closed his eyes and counted to ten, willing his phone to stop buzzing. Don't give in to her, don't answer the phone. To his relief, the phone fell silent, and he breathed out a sigh.

Looking up, he saw a table of young women staring at him and giggling. He smiled at them, and sure enough, a moment later, one of them dared to come over.

"Mr. Scamo?"

He stood and shook the young woman's hand. "Hey there." She flushed red with pleasure. He posed for a selfie with her and signed her notepad. She thanked him and went back to her table.

He was used to the attention. His name was well-known in celebrity circles now, thanks to his skill behind the camera.

Pilot Scamo, the son of a billionaire Italian city banker and an American feminist, was nearly forty now, but age had not withered his incredible looks. Intense green eyes, dark olive skin, and an unruly mop of wild dark curls meant he was catnip to women—and men—and people assumed he would be someone who slept around.

His ex-wife always assumed he was fucking the models and celebrities he shot for Vogue and Cosmo and so she had taken a myriad of lovers in their fifteen-year marriage. Pilot? Not once. He had been steadfastly faithful to Eugenie, even as she screwed her way through her Upper East Side friends' husbands, then his friends, his colleagues ... even his ex-best friend Wallis. Wally had been drunk, and devastated afterward, but Genie had crowed in Pilot's face.

Her cruelty had been her own way of loving him.

But, even now, three years after he'd finally had enough and divorced Genie, she still kept him on a string, using his kind nature against him, always playing the victim, the narcissist in her unleashed. She had been desperate to cling to him, proud to be on the arm of such a beautiful man, the envy of every woman.

Her cocaine habit had grown out of control, and now the rail-thin blonde was heading for some sort of crisis. But God help me, I can't be part of it, Pilot thought now. He rubbed his eyes and checked his watch. Nelly was late, of course. His old college buddy, now the publicist for one of America's most prestigious ballet companies, was irreverent, gossipy, and the complete opposite of Genie—the two women loathed each other and made no secret of it, and so he hadn't seen Nelly for nearly seven years. When she'd called him out of the blue and arranged a lunch at Gotan on Franklin Street, Pilot had been delighted.

He saw her now, barreling through the door, her messenger bag knocking a glass off a table, her musical laugh as she apologized to the server who came to help. Pilot grinned as he watched Nelly charm the young man, then she was hugging Pilot. "Gorgeous boy, how are you?"

Pilot kissed her cheek. "I'm good, thank you, Nel. Glad to see you again."

They sat down and Nelly unwound her scarf from her neck, studying him. "You look stressed. Maleficent still bugging you day and night?"

Pilot had to laugh. Nelly's disdain for Eugenie was biting and hilarious—or would be if it wasn't so on the money. "You know Genie."

"Unfortunately." Nelly grimaced. "She showed up to one of the company's benefits the other day with a dude who could have been your mini-me."

A curl of unease crept through Pilot's body. Jesus, really, Genie? She was determined to humiliate him at every turn. Nelly noticed his expression and her own softened. "Hey, for what it's worth, she was a laughing stock."

"That doesn't help." Pilot blew out his cheeks and fixed a smile on his face. "But let's get back to you. It's so good to see you, Nel."

She reached over and squeezed his hand. "You too, Pil. God, you get better looking every year—if only I was born liking dudes, I'd do you sideways."

Pilot snorted with laughter. "Sideways? How exactly would that work?"

"You dare to question me?" Nelly grinned. "How's work?"

Pilot's smile faded. "Slow. I have an exhibit coming up at MOMA, to benefit the Quilla Chen Foundation ... Grady Mallory offered it to me, but I haven't got anything. Not anything." He tapped his head. "Nothing is going on up here; the juice isn't flowing. I spend my days just wandering around the city, hoping something will trigger an idea."

"Hobo."

Pilot smiled. "Brainless hobo, at the moment."

"Well, I may be able to help."

They were interrupted then by the waiter who took their order, grilled cheese for Pilot, a cauliflower and tahini sandwich for Nelly, a lifelong vegetarian. As Pilot sipped his coffee, he raised his eyebrows at Nelly. "So?"

"The Company is struggling," she said matter-of-factly. "Since Oona's suicide, and the crap in the paper about Kristof, our funding has dropped significantly."

"I read about that … so that stuff about Kristof isn't true?"

"Oh, no," Nelly shook her head, "it's all true. He is a junkie and a cheating asshole, but he's also a genius artistic director. Really, he couldn't be more clichéd if he tried, but Oliver Fortuna is determined to keep hold of him."

"Who is Fortuna?"

Nelly smiled. "Our founder. God bless him, he's wonderful, and he's intensely loyal." She sighed. "Too loyal, sometimes. Anyway, I digress. We were talking about ways to up our profile without referencing Kristof's past, and a photographic exhibit of our dancers, shot by one of the best photographers in the work—you—would be a great start. Then, we're working towards a major performance of work, called La Petite Morte. Kristof is putting it together—it's an excerpt from erotic ballets with a dark twist."

Pilot was nodding, but he wasn't enthused. "I'm happy to help but it's been done, recently too."

"Wait until you see our dancers—there are one or two of them who transcend ballet. That's all I'll say now because I want you to find your muse in our company. Pilot, you were the first person I thought of for this—I've seen you get that glint in your eye when something or someone inspires you." She squeezed his cheek, grinning. "Trust me on this—you will find it at NYSMBC."

. . .

LATER, as he walked home to his penthouse flat, he wondered about the job. The New York State and Metropolitan Ballet Company. He knew very little about dance, but Nelly had been their chief of publicity for many years, and he'd occasionally photographed their shows for them.

Kristof Mendelev was another matter. Pilot's dealings with the man had only ever been negative—Mendelev had been one of Eugenie's myriad lovers and had boasted about it whenever Pilot had been to one of their functions. He knew the ex-ballet dancer was loathed by his colleagues, but like Nelly had told him, Kristof was a genius on the ballet stage. Feted by every major ballet company around the world, Kristof knew his worth.

"He's the reason we're struggling cash-wise," Nelly had told Pilot. "His salary is six figures, but he has to submit to weekly drug-testing. That's the one unbreakable condition of his employment. So far—he's clean."

Pilot had told Nelly he would happily photograph the dancers for the company but he didn't hold faith that it would be the key to unlocking his inspiration. When he got home, he checked his voicemails. Grady Mallory, just checking in. Pilot deleted that message guiltily. One message from his mom, Blair, asking him to call her. Three from his younger half-sister Romana, herself an up-and-coming photographer, and finally, seven messages from Eugenie, each more hysterical than the last.

Don't give in to her. Don't call her back.

Pilot sighed and flicked through his contacts, pressing the dial button. After a second, he heard her voice—and smiled. "Hey, little sis," he said, his tone warm and loving, "what gives?"

CHAPTER TWO

Boheme Dali battered her shoes against the stone wall, trying to break them in. She thought she had done so last night, hours of bending and stretching the shoes, but, as always with new shoes, they'd wrecked her feet after only one ballet class.

She looked up as a female voice called her name, and smiled. Grace Hardacre, one of the guest performers this year, came to sit down by her in the corridor outside the studio. "Hey, Boh."

"Hey yourself. How's mentoring going?" Grace was mentoring an apprentice of the ballet company's in addition to performing with them.

Grace smiled. "Lexie is incredible," she said warmly, "and such a sponge. I tell her one thing and she gets it."

Boheme smiled. She remembered what it had been like to be an apprentice, even one with her talent; she was still put through the ringer by her tutor, former prima ballerina, Celine Peletier, who was now her champion and a formidable teacher at the company. It had made her the dancer she was today.

Grace nodded at her shoes. "The one constant in ballet—painful shoes. New?"

"Yup." Boheme grimaced as she saw blood in the toe of them. "God, Liquid Skin, here I come." She dragged the tube of liquid bandage from her bag.

Grace looked sympathetic. "Ouch."

Boheme shrugged. "But necessary. Anyway, what brings you over here?" She sucked in a breath as she applied the liquid to her toes.

"The douche wishes to see me about the workshop. I think he wants me on his side about what ballets he wants to do."

"Ah. They're still fighting over The Lesson?"

"Yup. Liz thinks it's misogynist and too violent, whereas Kristof says that's the point of the whole sex and death thing he's got going on."

Boheme rolled her eyes. "I hate to say this, but I kind of get where he's coming from." She bent over as far as she could and blew on her toes.

"Me too, but Liz argues Mayerling or La Sylphide cover the same ground."

"Well, she's right, but isn't that point of this workshop? We're doing three excerpts from three different stories." Boh sighed. "Well, whatever. It's not like we haven't plenty of tragic ballets to choose from. Although I have to admit, I'm relieved not to have to do Romeo and Juliet again."

Grace chuckled. "You've always hated that one. People love it."

"It's not a love story," Boh said, "it's a stupid teen angst story."

"Philistine."

"Boring."

They both laughed and Grace help Boh get to her feet. "Come on, let's grab something to eat before we go home."

Boh and Grace shared a walk-up apartment in Brooklyn and

had done so since they were both in the corps de ballet. Now that they were both senior dancers, they could have afforded their own places, but they enjoyed living with each other and saw no reason to change.

They ate at a small diner on the way to the subway, then huddled down together as the train took them home. September and the heat of the New York summer had quickly faded and as fall began, the leaves were falling and a cold wind from the north was swirling around the city.

At home, their cat, Beelzebub, a darkly malevolent tabby, was waiting for them to feed him, wandering between their legs, yelling until Boh dumped a bowl of kibble on the kitchen floor for him. "Fiend," she said fondly, scratching his ears as he ate his food.

Grace had a date, and so, after commandeering the bathroom for an hour, she called goodbye to Boh, who was reading in her room. The apartment was silent after Grace left, and Boh reveled in the peace of it. She loved being alone, away from other people, the long hours of exercise and practice a strain on her introverted side

She loved ballet, every part of it except the public side. Boh had been raised to be quiet, the silent child at the dinner table, the only-speak-when-spoken-to daughter. The youngest of five, Boh had often been forgotten by her wayward parents, who only had children because it was expected of them in their Indian American family. The moment she was sixteen, Boh had taken the money she had saved from her part-time job at the local Dairy Queen and caught a bus to New York City. She had lived on fellow dancers' couches until she was accepted into her ballet school, then stayed in the dorm rooms, where she had met Grace.

Now in her own place, her family a distant memory, Boh was as content as she had ever been—apart from one glaring thing.

Lately, she had experienced fatigue for many days in a row. Days turned into weeks, and finally, last week she had been to see her doctor. She had anemia, probably, her doctor told her, hereditary. "A mild version, thank goodness, and we can treat you." The doctor smiled kindly at her as she read through her notes. "I already know the answer to this, Boh, but could you see yourself taking some time off?"

They had both laughed, but they both knew there was zero chance of that. "I'll take any pills, eat anything you say I should, but that's the one thing I can't do. I will get as much rest as I can, I promise." Boh told her, and the doctor had to be satisfied with that.

Boh got up now and went to run a bath. She thought herself lucky that her naturally introverted nature meant she rarely went out at night, preferring to stay home and read or watch movies. She and Grace would sometimes cook for each other, healthy, made-from-scratch meals from recipes they found on the Internet, otherwise a usual diet of salmon or chicken with steamed vegetables was their mainstay.

Despite the rumors of eating disorders plaguing the ballet world, it was less prevalent than expected and the NYSMBC had strict policies on nutrition. "Fit, healthy bodies of appropriate weight for age and height" was the mantra. When a dancer was suspected of developing a disorder, they were given three strikes to help combat it, and support to beat it. If the dancer didn't do their part, after three sessions with the company counselor, they were dismissed from the company and sent to a treatment center. The company's chief executive, Liz Secretariat, an ex-prima, enforced that rule fiercely, and chastised any teacher who made the dancers question their body shape.

Of course, it didn't mean the dancers could gorge themselves, but now, when Boh broke off a large piece of dark chocolate and put it on a plate to enjoy as she soaked in the bath, she didn't feel guilty about it. She downed two of her prescribed iron tablets with some orange juice and grabbed her old half-buried-beneath-paperbacks copy of her company guidelines. She still didn't know whether she was required to report her illness if it wasn't serious. She would rather not. It would just mean the company watching her closely and she could do without that right now.

She wished Kristof, the company's art director, would make up his mind about which ballets to perform. It made rehearsals stressful when they were running through six or seven different combinations to vastly different music. All of the dancers' feet were wrecked, but Kristof seemed to work Boh harder than the rest. While they caught their breath, he would tell Boh to run through a set of leaps and jumps, basic steps that even the apprentices knew.

After the sessions, he would keep her longer to tell her about every single step she had performed, what was wrong with it, what was wrong with her. Boh had a thick skin and she would automatically filter out the nonsense and concentrate on the stuff that she could learn from.

Of course, when Kristof was in an extra-spiteful mood, even her thick skin couldn't escape his barbs. That, she knew, stemmed from her refusal to sleep with him. More than once he had come onto her, and every time she said no. It wasn't just that she had no interest in him sexually, but the thought of his hands on her body made her feel sick.

She knew some of her fellow dancers found him attractive, and looking at the man with an unbiased eye, she knew he was a handsome man. Dark hair, dark brown eyes, a square, strong jaw … yes, Kristof Mendelev was a catch.

But she loathed his personality, his arrogance, even though his high opinion of his own talent was justified. Boh was so aware of the important of confidence tempered with humility that she couldn't abide conceit.

Serena, her fellow dancer and nemesis, would scoff at her. "You're too soft, Dali. This is ballet—it doesn't get more cutthroat than this."

"And yet, still, I made principal without having to resort to being a bitch, Serena," she would shoot back to the amusement of the other dancers.

Her hated of Serena went deeper than being rivals for the leading roles. Boh knew she had the edge—but so did Serena, and that made the other woman antagonistic. Not only that, but Boh suspected Serena of being racist. Boh was the first Indian American to become principal in their ballet company, and the company had made much in the media of her ascendance. Serena, an Upper East Side princess, had mocked the interviews and photo shoots, but Boh knew it was only out of jealousy.

Serena was a thorn in her side but not a big one. As Boh soaked in the tub, she tried to concentrate on her book—the new Paul Auster—but found her mind wandering. Today she had received a letter from her oldest sister, Maya, telling her that their father was seriously ill and not likely to live another six months.

Boh tested her heart and felt nothing. Nothing for the man who'd ignored her for the first seven years of her life, and then, on her eighth birthday, the day they had moved into a new apartment and she had her own room for once, the day he had crept into her room for what he would call their "Special Secret Time."

No, she felt nothing for the man who had abused her. She had told only one person—Maya—who had slapped her face and told her never to tell. Boheme knew, at that moment, that her father had done the same thing to her sister.

Bastard.

She had written back to Maya.

I'm sorry for the pain it causes the rest of you, but really, he gets what he deserves. You know why.
Boh.

There had been no reply and now Boh pushed the memories of her father away. You, she thought, you are the reason I have no heart, no passion for a man. You.

She hauled herself out of the cool water and studied her naked body in front of the mirror. Tall, lean, with skin the color of milky coffee, she nevertheless had full breasts, something Serena mocked her for too, but she never worried that she didn't fit the preferred dancer body type. It wasn't such a big deal, nowadays.

She dried herself off and changed into her worn but comfortable pajamas, slipping into bed and switching off the lamp. It was only 10 p.m. but she didn't care. Sleep was ambrosia to her, especially now. God, I am middle-aged at twenty-two, she thought to herself, but soon her eyes closed and she fell into a peaceful sleep, woken only by Beelzebub padding his paws onto her back in the early hours.

"You little asshole," she said, then smiled as he curled up on the pillow next to her and immediately stretched his leg over her face. She removed it gently and kissed his tiny paw. "You're the only man for me, Beez," she whispered, then closed her eyes and slept until her alarm sounded at seven a.m. the next morning.

CHAPTER THREE

"I can't remember—have you been inside this building before?" Nelly asked Pilot as he arrived with his Polaroid camera—he was old school when it came to initial scouting—two weeks after their lunch in the city. He'd moved things around, avoiding calls from Grady Mallory until he could no longer put it off. He'd had to make something up on the fly to tell Grady. "It's a study of the human body in movement," he said. "I'm visiting with the New York State and Metro Ballet to see their ballerinas at work.

He didn't blame Grady for sounding less than enthusiastic. Ballet dancers in movement had been done before, many, many times, but Grady, being the nice guy that he was, nevertheless thanked Pilot for his ideas.

Pilot felt bad about his lack of direction. "Look, Gray, I promise I'll come up with something spectacular."

"I have faith," Grady had told him. Pilot hoped he could repay that faith.

Following Nelly into the ballet company's building, he shook his head. "No, not this one, but the old one down on Bleecker."

"Ha, yeah, that's a story. That building was just condemned

... asbestos. We dodged a bullet there, selling it before it was discovered. Anyway, where do you want to start? Do you want to meet the dancers or just look in on a class?"

"Just look in, if that's all right. I just need to see who I'm going to be shooting."

"In that case," Nelly directed him into the elevator, "there's a mixed class you should see. Principals down to apprentices. Celine likes to hold a two-hour long class on Monday mornings which is more about fine-tuning than it is rehearsing for anything specific. Very good for building comradery in the company. Everyone loves it, as you can imagine, although they're all terrified of Celine."

Pilot grinned. His own mother was a strident, effusive, strong woman, and he'd inherited a love of powerful women—powerful, not manipulative. "How is the comradery?"

Nelly laughed. "What you would expect. For the most part, they're a friendly bunch, but there's always one or two assholes."

"Who should I look out for?"

Nelly chuckled. "I shouldn't say."

"Go on, gossip a little."

She sighed. "Serena. A Grade 1 uber-bitch. Fantastic dancer, of course, but a harridan. Jeremy can be a diva."

"You play favorites?"

"I don't teach them so I can." She gave him a mischievous look. "Boh. You'll love Boh. Lexie, Grace, Vlad, Elliott, Fernanda ... look, most of them. Just look out for Serena, Jeremy, and maybe even Alex."

"Good info, thanks."

They stepped out of the elevator and Nelly pointed him towards the studio. "I told Celine to expect you."

Pilot chuckled. "You know me so well."

He opened the door to the studio a crack and caught the eyes of the fierce-looking woman inside. She nodded, unsmiling, and nodded her head to the front of the class.

Pilot slipped inside, his eyes sweeping over the dancers inside. A couple looked at him curiously, but most were focused on their practice. A young man, around Pilot's age, was playing the piano. He looked up and smiled at Pilot.

"And up, good. Arms lifted ... Lexie, extend, please ... beautiful. Alex, turn out ... good. Lovely stretch, Boh, well done. Double pirouette, no, Elliot, double. Thank you."

Pilot listened to her guiding her pupils through the class. He had to admit, the way they used their bodies to form shapes was beautiful and impressive. He squatted at the front and took some shots. A dancer with pale, red-gold hair in a tight bun on the top of her head caught his eye and smiled seductively, posing for him.

"Serena, pay attention to me and not Mr. Scamo, please, no matter how pretty he is."

Pilot gave a snort of laughter and Celine glared at him, winking to show she was kidding. He liked her immediately.

"Okay, and rest. Thank you. Well, as Serena has noticed, we have a visitor. For those of you who live under a rock, this is Pilot Scamo, photographer extraordinaire." Celine came over to shake Pilot's hand as the assembled group gave him a small round of applause. He felt his face flame—he never got used to being the center of attention.

"Hey everyone, listen, I'm just here to capture the action, so please, don't let me interrupt ..." Pilot's voice faltered as he saw her. The tall, athletic woman standing a little way behind a male dancer. She was looking at him shyly, her dark brown eyes large, her body all curves and yet athletic and toned. She was luminous. Pilot realized he was staring and quickly looked away. "Sorry, um, don't let me interrupt you."

Celine hid a smile. "You heard the man. Right, next combination. In fourth, then plié, relevé, plié ..."

Pilot continued his shooting while the dancers practiced. After working at the barre, Celine had them showcase their leaps and jumps for him. "And, Boh, if you could finish for us with your triple pirouette and into arabesque."

At the end of the jetés, his girl stepped forward, all grace, and executed a flawless pirouette and finished in the classic pose of arabesque. Every line of her body was exquisite, down to the placement of her fingers. Pilot sucked in a deep breath.

He had found his muse.

CHAPTER FOUR

As Boh left the studio, she couldn't help glancing back at the man talking to Celine. The way he had looked at her ... if any other man had looked at her like that, she would have frozen, gotten distressed, and panicked. But this man ...

It was his eyes. Bright green, and large, his thick dark brows making them intense, dangerous, sensual. A line between his brows made it look as if he was frowning or troubled until he smiled. Then his entire face lit up, became boyish, almost beautiful. He was the sexiest man she had ever seen, and she felt it everywhere.

Lexie nudged her. "Somebody made an impression."

Boh grinned at her and lowered her voice. "So you noticed too?"

"Everyone noticed, Boh. It was almost a cartoon double-take he did. And he's gorgeous too."

"Old enough to be your father," Serena butted in, obviously listening to them as they made their way to the changing rooms. "And you, Dali, don't go thinking you're something special just because a man gave you the eye. He's a superstar—he's probably had more supermodels in the last week than you've had successful triple pirouettes."

"Serena, your bitch is showing." Fernanda, the mild-mannered guest dancer from Ecuador spoke then, and Serena flushed with anger, muttering something under her breath. Fernanda stopped and gripped Serena's shoulder. "What did you say?"

Serena smiled nastily. "You heard." She wrenched her shoulder from Fernanda's grip and stalked off. Boh sighed. Serena's attitude had gotten even worse lately, and she wondered why Fernanda had got involved. It wasn't like her. She looked questioningly at her friend now and Fernanda shrugged.

"Sometimes she just needs to hear shut the fuck up from someone new, you know."

Boh and Lexie laughed and Fernanda grinned. "Come on. We'll be late for Kristof."

AFTER THE NOISE of the class, the studio rang with silence as Pilot laid out his Polaroids on top of the piano and studied them. He noted down several of the dancers he'd like to photograph, choosing them for the clean lines of their bodies, but really, he was trying not to concentrate on the last three pictures.

Boheme. Boh. The way her body moved through the air, her curves made as gracefully as the pin-thin dancers. Strong, athletic, and almost otherworldly. He knew enough about ballet to know her body type wasn't the preferred willowy waif. Her body was all woman, the result of a finely tuned workout program, he guessed, along with a healthy appetite. He found her thrilling. Her poise and grace were reflected in the natural beauty of her face, devoid of make-up and with a fine, dewy sheen of sweat making the light sparkle from her …

Calm down, man. Pilot sucked in a deep breath but his

stomach was in knots. The old feeling. When he knew he'd found someone who could radiate sensuality, strength, and above all artistry through his lens. He would gladly photograph the rest of the dancers for the company, to help with their publicity, but he would ask Boh to work with him for his exhibition.

He went to find Nelly, who was delighted he had enjoyed the class. "The dancers are astonishing," he said honestly, sitting down on her desk. "There were a few who really stood out ... here." He handed her a set of six Polaroids and she sorted through them, nodding.

"Grace, Lexie, Jeremy, Vlad, Fernanda, and Elliott. Oh." She looked up at him curiously and he knew what she was thinking. He grinned and handed her the last three Polaroids.

"I said they stood out. But there was one who blew the rest out of the water."

He saw Nelly's shoulders relax as she looked at the pictures of Boh. She nodded and smiled. "I knew it. I knew you would like her. She's something else."

"That she is," he said and Nelly chuckled.

"Crushing?"

Pilot pretended to look affronted. "Please, I'm a professional. I'm also a man, and who could blame me? But seriously ... I have a proposition."

Nelly gave him a mischievous grin. "God, we're not talking Pygmalion, are we? I already have Machiavelli on staff."

"Ha, no, not quite. Listen, I told you about the Chen Foundation exhibit?"

"You did ... ah, I see. You want Boh to be your muse?"

Pilot nodded. "If she'll agree. It would mean working around her ballet schedule, of course, and she may not want to put in the extra hours. I'll pay her, of course ... and on top of that, I'll do your publicity shots free of charge."

Nelly's eyes bugged. "No, Pilot, I couldn't …"

"Look at my eyes," he said, with a grin, "If you can tell me you've seen me more excited about a project than this, I take it all back."

A slow smile spread across Nelly's face. "Okay, you're on … if Boh agrees."

"Of course, absolutely. But I'll do your stuff for free anyway." It wasn't as if he needed the money and as far as Pilot was concerned, Nelly had given him his mojo back and there was no price on that.

Nelly looked at the clock. "Well, Boh's in with Kristof at the moment. I could pull her."

"No, don't interrupt her class."

Nelly snorted. "It would piss Kristof off though, and everyone would enjoy that. Come on, let's go see if we can steal her away."

KRISTOF MENDELEV STARED at Boh as she moved through the mime section of La Sylphide and then stopped her. "Boh, this isn't a sarcastic rendition, nor is it a cartoon. Subtly is key in this part of the dance. If you break out and make the audience laugh then you're doing a disservice to the sensuality of the moment."

Boh stood silently as he critiqued her then asked coolly, "Shall I try it again?"

"What else are we here for? Of course, try again."

She moved across the floor, her port de bras moving in graceful arcs, her feet moving swiftly across the floor, fast and staccato in the style made famous by the ballet's choreographer August Bournonville. Boh knew this ballet better than most of the others, having loved it since she was a child. She loved being the fairy, the sylph, and so her body bent and curved to every note of the music. This time she played the mime earnestly, reaching out with her love across the forest where the fairies dwelled, proclaiming her love for James, the hapless hero of the ballet. Vladimir, Boh's fellow principal, played James, moving with her, and Boh lost herself in the movements.

As she played out La Sylphide's dying moments, her focus shifted back into the room and she saw Pilot Scamo watching her.

"Okay, stop." Kristof was rubbing his head and glaring at Nelly. "Is there some reason for this intrusion? How is she—" he gestured rudely towards Boh, "—going to get any better if we keep being interrupted?"

Nelly didn't rise to the bait. "I told you about this earlier, Kris. Were you listening?"

But he wasn't listening now; he was staring at Pilot, who gazed back coolly. "Well, if it isn't Scamo." He said his name with accompanying jazz hands, mocking Pilot. Pilot's eyes looked dangerous and Boh shivered, but he didn't take the bait. Pilot's eyes met hers and softened and his mouth hitched up on one side.

"Miss Dali," he said, his tone respectful and admiring, "looked exquisite to me."

Boh flushed with pleasure and then a snigger went through the class until Kristof glared at them.

Kristof rolled his eyes. "What do you want?"

"We'd like to talk to Boh, please. In private."

"And it couldn't wait until after my class?"

"Obviously not." Nelly's voice took on a dangerous note and Kristof stared her down for a moment, obviously deciding whether to argue his case. Eventually he gave a sharp nod of the head to Boh, who stepped out gracefully of the troupe and came towards them, gathering her bag and towel, shooting an apologetic look at the rest of her class.

. . .

Outside, Nelly introduced them. "Boheme Dali, meet Pilot Scamo. Not that he needs introducing."

"And after what I saw this morning, neither do you, Miss Dali." He shook her hand and smiled at her.

"It's Boh, please." Her voice was quiet and soft, musical. Nelly grinned at them both, obviously noticing the forming connection between them.

"Pilot," he said and Nelly patted his back.

"I'll leave you two alone to talk. Pilot has a very interesting proposition for you, Boh."

She disappeared and Pilot smiled at Boh. "Shall we take a walk? I don't much feel like having an audience." He nodded inside the dance studio where Kristof was watching them and Boh nodded, rolling her eyes.

"Good idea. I know somewhere we can go for some privacy."

She took him down to the bottom of the building and out of the kitchen area to a small courtyard. "No one comes down here much unless it's to smoke, but class is in session so we should have some privacy." She shivered a little at the cold breeze.

"Here." Pilot shrugged out of his jacket and put it around her shoulders. She smiled at him gratefully.

"Thank you." They sat down at one of the picnic benches. "It really is an honor to meet you, sir."

Pilot grinned. "My dad was 'sir,' Boh, I'm just Pilot. And likewise. Nelly told me you were special and I believe she underplayed that statement. You move like—" he cast around for the word, "—like water, like air ... Boh, Nell mentioned a proposition and here it is. I'm scheduled to work with the Quilla Chen Foundation for an exhibit at MOMA in six weeks. Before this morning, I had nothing. No juices were getting to my brain, no inspiration, no nothing. Then I saw you dance."

Boh's face was flaming red. Pilot Scamo was inspired ... by her? No way. No freakin' way. Pilot's name was known all over the world and he'd photographed some of the world's most beautiful women—Serena's jibe about him sleeping with supermodels came back to her.

"Mr. Scamo—"

"Pilot."

"Pilot—what exactly is it that you're asking me to do?" If this was a line to get her into bed—God help her but this gorgeous man wouldn't need a line—she would have to revise her good opinion of him.

"Work with me on this project. Obviously, we'll need a theme, and my ideas are at the very early stages. I'm sure you've seen the many, many ballet portraits that have been done already; photographers like Karolina Kuras or Alexander Yakovlev have produced some stunning work. So we need an original angle. I'd like to work with you and figure something out."

"In six weeks?"

Pilot nodded. "In six weeks we'd have to come up with a theme, get the costumes, find the settings." He smiled suddenly, a wide, boyish smile, and Boh felt her belly quiver with desire. Working closely together with this man for six weeks? Yes, please ...

"I'm in." She found herself saying and was reward by an even bigger, even sexier smile.

"Fantastic."

They swapped contact details and Boh smiled shyly at him. "I guess we're going to have to start right away."

"I guess so." His eyes dropped to her mouth for a split second and then he looked away, a faint spot of pink appearing on each of his cheeks. Boh realized he didn't want to look like a creep, but there was no denying the attraction between them. Still, this man was a professional and so was she.

But, at least, she thought later, after she'd said goodbye, I have a new friend. Ha, her body said to her, when was the last time you got wet over a friend?

Shut up. But she grinned to herself as she made her way back up to Kristof's class, feeling lighter than air at the thought of spending the next six weeks with Pilot Scamo.

CHAPTER FIVE

Pilot's good mood lasted until he got back to his apartment and saw his doorman shifting uncomfortably from foot to foot. "Mister Scamo," he said, "I'm sorry. She wouldn't take no for an answer. She's waiting upstairs."

Pilot sighed. "It's not your fault, Ben. It's okay."

Eugenie was sitting outside his apartment door and Pilot was grateful that he had never given in to her request for a key. "Why?" he had asked when Eugenie suggested it, "We're divorced, Genie."

She saw him now and held her hands out to him so he helped her up. She didn't let go of his hands, instead pressing them around her waist. "Darling."

Pilot gently extracted himself. "Genie, what are you doing here?"

Eugenie huffed. "Well, if you don't want to see me."

God, it was going to be one of those days. She really was the queen of passive-aggressiveness. "I'm working, Genie. As I said, what is it that you want?"

"To see you, obviously." She stroked a hand down his face

and it was all Pilot could do not to jerk his head away. He'd been there before and knew what the consequences of that would be. The half-moon scar next to right eye was evidence of Genie's rage when she was slighted. "I miss you, Pilot. More than you know."

Ah, Genie Ploy number three, he thought. The regretful ex. "Genie, you've been calling me nonstop and as I said, I'm working. You know what it's like when I have a project on."

He was hoping to keep the argument out in the hallway, but as one of his neighbors edged along the corridor, curious, and not being shy about it, Pilot opened his door and stepped back to allow Eugenie to enter. Damn it. He had been successfully keeping her away from his new life until now.

Genie walked into his apartment and smiled. "Ah, typical Pilot. Unorganized mess."

He shrugged. Eugenie liked everything in its place all the time; Pilot wanted his home to look lived in by a human, not an automaton. His walls were lined with bookshelves stuffed to the gills, his couch was old and battered and incredibly comfortable, his record player was on the floor with a stack of vinyl next to it. On the coffee table, a collection of mugs had varying degrees of old coffee or tea; a half-empty bottle of scotch, a notebook with ideas.

But Genie was wrong—Pilot knew where every single piece of his life fit in this place—it was his haven and he hated that she was in it, judging it, sneering at it.

"Like I said, many times now, I'm working, so—" He made a motion for her to say what she had to say. Genie half-smiled. She was looking even thinner these days. Always slim, when he had met her she had been a healthy weight but as the years went on, she lost her appetite for anything but vodka and cocaine, and when Pilot had left her, her addictions had only gotten worse. Now she looked to be under 100 pounds.

Of course, Genie herself didn't mind the weight loss at all. In her circle of Upper East Side friends, she was the thinnest, could fit into the sample sizes of all the best fashion designers, and reveled in her addictions. Apart from cocaine, Adderall, and the occasional speedball, she would start every day using meth. Her fragile, brittle blonde beauty was already beginning to crack at the seams. Pilot would have felt sorry for her but her cruelty made him feel numb to her downfall.

"My darling," she came toward him now and he couldn't help but back up a few paces. She noticed and anger flashed in her eyes, but she struggled and smiled. "Don't be scared of me, my darling. Pilot, after everything, the life we built, the love we had, don't you think we deserve more than this, this sad little divorce?"

"We've discussed this before, Genie, when you weren't high. We both know it's over. It has been for years. Maybe, it should never have even started."

Genie ignored him. "We never tried for children because of your career, and so now, I think it's time."

Oh God, she really was on one of her diatribes. Pilot rubbed his face. How am I going to get her out of my apartment without her losing her shit on me—again?

"Genie, I have a meeting I have to get to. Go home, sober up, and you'll realize the nonsense you're talking. We're divorced. No children. Not from me."

He took her shoulders and steered her out of the apartment, feeling how bony and frail her body felt. "Goodbye, Genie." The last he saw of her, her mouth was flapping uselessly, like a goldfish as she blinked in astonishment at her speedy banishment.

He shut the door quickly and leaned back against it. It wasn't that he was afraid of her—he was more afraid of the repercussions if she attacked him again. He was three times her weight and size—if he fought back and hurt her, he knew which side the police would come down on and it wouldn't be his. Plus, her family had connections. The Ratcliffe-Morgans were old money, not the 'nouveau riche' of men like his father, a self-made billionaire, and during their marriage, Eugenie had made it very cleared that his money was inferior. She hated that he made no attempt to battle the prenup, that he wasn't interested in money at all. It gave her one less thing to hold over him.

Now, his buzz from earlier destroyed, Pilot grabbed his bag and dug out the Polaroids, wanting to get back some of the excitement he had felt. He flicked through the photographs and found the ones of Boh. A warmth replaced the anxiety in his stomach. He snagged his phone from his jacket and sent her a message.

Really excited to be working with you, Boh. Pilot.

He hadn't expected her to reply so quickly and when he saw her message, he smiled.

You too! I've just been on the Internet to research some stuff—you are the king of Pinterest! Looking forward to starting work. B.

Sweet. Pilot glanced at the clock. Just after six p.m. He hesitated for a moment then typed in another message. Have you eaten yet?

Not yet, I just got out of rehearsal.

Pilot drew in a deep breath. Was this inappropriate? Ah, to hell with it.

Feel like grabbing a burger and getting started?

He counted the second before she replied. Sounds good. Where should I meet you?

Pilot couldn't help the victorious "Yes" that escaped his lips.

CHAPTER SIX

"The seasons."

"Been done."

"Um ... the elements?"

"Also done."

"Dang it." Boh shoved another bite of burger into her mouth and screwed up her face. Pilot grinned at her, a blob of mustard on the side of his own mouth. Without thinking, she reached over and swept it off with her finger. Immediately getting that it was a very intimate thing to do to someone she didn't know, she flushed, but Pilot just smiled and thanked her.

To cover her embarrassment, she made a joke of it. "I did contemplate leaving it there and letting you walk out of here, but I thought it was too early in our working relationship to do that."

Pilot laughed—God, his smile was intoxicating. "Well, I'm glad you thought so ... because now I can tell you about the ketchup on your cheek."

Boh's eyes widened, and she scrubbed furiously at both of her cheeks with the sleeve of her sweater. She checked but there was no ketchup on the fabric. Pilot gave her his best cheesy grin.

"Kidding."

Boh giggled. Over the last hour, she had learned that Pilot had the same goofy sense of humor that she did, and although she had been nervous when they first met up, now she was having a great time. They'd talked about the project and now Pilot had his notebook out in front of him.

"I thought we could just spitball ideas until we come up with a theme," he'd said after they'd ordered their food. They were at Bubby's on Hudson Street, and Boh was eating the most sublime burger she'd ever tasted, a mid-rare burger with fries. She'd skipped lunch—well, she'd been forced to skip lunch when Kristof made her make up for missing so much of his class—and now she was ravenous.

It didn't hurt that her view was so pleasant. Pilot, dressed in a dark navy sweater, his hair wild about his head, a dark five-o-clock shadow on his handsome face, was talking about themes and they were trying to think of something original.

"How about a ballerina in urban decay settings?"

Boh considered. "I do like that idea, but there's also a growing trend of urban ballet and I wonder if we could run into trouble there."

Pilot was tapping into his phone. "Yeah, you're right and of course, it's—"

"Already been done?"

Pilot chuckled. "Yep. Damn, I thought we had this."

Boh smiled shyly at him. "Come on, we've barely started. So, no elements, seasons, city dumps …"

Pilot laughed. "And, please, God, no star signs."

"Amen to that." Boh stuck a French fry into her mouth. He was so easy to be with.

Pilot studied her. "What's Kristof's workshop about?"

"Sex and Death is the theme. He's pushing to do the murder

scene in The Lesson as part of the performance. Celine and Liz are fighting him."

"I don't know the ballet."

Boh leaned forward, in her element talking about her art, her passion. "The Lesson is the story of a teacher and his pupil. He's obsessed with her and during one particular lesson, he becomes more and more aroused by her performance until finally he snaps and stabs her to death."

Pilot grimaced. "Delightful."

Boh laughed. "Actually, when performed in the context of obsessive love, it is quite beautiful. The idea of being so in love with someone that you'd hurt them is something a lot of ballets cover. Mayerling, for example." She saw the strange look pass over his face. "What is it?"

He shook his head. "It's just ... the reality of that kind of relationship. There's nothing romantic about it."

She wondered who had hurt this beautiful man but didn't feel she could ask him directly. "Are you married, Pilot?"

"Divorced. Happily so."

Boh studied her fingernails. "Girlfriend?"

He didn't answer for a moment and she looked up to find him smiling at her, his eyes soft. "No, no girlfriend. You?"

She shook her head. Pilot leaned forward and gently brushed his lips against hers then drew back, his eyes searching hers. "Was that okay?"

Boh was having a hard job catching her breath. "More than okay," she whispered, and Pilot chuckled and kissed her again.

"You realize," he murmured against her lips, "that I'm just relieving you of ketchup and mustard. You have it all over your face."

They kissed again, and Boh's palms cupped her face, stroking the soft skin above his beard. *Ask me to come home with you* and I will, she silently asked him, shocking herself, but he made no attempt to try to talk her into his bed and she found herself warming to him. Yes, there was damage there, she thought, but Pilot Scamo was different to most men. She felt, in her bones, that he didn't want to take from her and that was new to her.

They talked some more but couldn't find an idea. "Let's call it a night," he said. "You look bushed. Can I drive you home?"

She got into his comfortable Mercedes and noted how worn it looked. Worn but comfortable, like an old friend. She knew nothing about cars, but the fact that he wasn't prissy about his made her smile. He saw her expression. "What?"

She told him and he laughed. "Yeah, she's just an old jalopy, really, but she's been very faithful to me."

"Can I ask you something?"

"Sure?"

"You come from money?"

Pilot nodded. "I can say that, yes, but there was a time before my dad made his money that I remember very well. Fifty-cent noodles from the bodega and cereal for dinner. My mom, she's a tenured professor at Columbia, but back then she was working her way up, plus bringing up a teenager and a baby, while Dad was working all hours at his company."

"What work did he do?"

"Really want to know?" Pilot gave her a grin, and she chuckled.

"As long as it's not gun-running."

"You might wish it was when I tell you."

Boh smiled. "Amaze me."

"Well," Pilot steered the car onto the Brooklyn Bridge, "You know those little perforations in toilet paper? My dad invented the perfect 'tear-rate'."

Boh blinked. That was the last thing she'd expected to hear. "Really?"

Pilot slid his eyes over to her. "Nope."

For a second Boh didn't comprehend what he'd said, then she busted out laughing. "You had me. You really had me."

Pilot chuckled. "Well, it was a more interesting line than he worked real hard in the city and made a wad of cash."

"You are quite insane, Pilot Scamo." She giggled, shaking her head.

They joked with each other on the way back to her apartment, then he walked her to her door. "Goodnight, Boheme Dali."

He kissed her gently, and she smiled. "Goodnight, Pilot. Thank you for dinner, for driving me home, and—thank you."

He stroked her cheek. "May I call you tomorrow?"

She nodded, and he kissed her one more time before he waved goodbye.

Boh went inside to find Grace asleep on the couch, Beelzebub curled on top of her head, awake, watching Boh with baleful eyes. "You're just jealous I got to kiss a gorgeous man," she whispered, draping a blanket over Grace's sleeping form.

When she was in bed, all she could think about was Pilot's kiss, his sweet smile, his touch, and she wished she were curled up next to him right now.

When she slept, she dreamed of dancing into his arms and never leaving that loving embrace. When she woke, she woke to a text message of two words.

Lightning bolt.

CHAPTER SEVEN

"I wasn't being cheesy, I swear, but it just came to me. I was thinking about meeting you, and then when I got home, some hokey rom-com movie was on cable. That one with the guy with the floppy hair, says fuck a lot."

Boh giggled. "Four Weddings and a Funeral?"

"That's the one." Pilot sipped his coffee. "Well, right at the very end, there's that meeting between the sick-kick guy and the posh woman, and there's this frisson. He even says it 'Gosh, thunderbolt city.' Are you laughing at my English accent?"

"No, no." Boh stuck her tongue in her cheek. Had she only known this man for 24 hours? Plot flicked a crumb of her bagel at her and she grinned. "So, carry on."

"Heard of Faraday cages?"

Boh screwed up her face. "Should I have?"

"Ah, the youth of today. Anyway, ignoramus, a Faraday cage is a kind of enclosure which will shield things, a human, anything from electricity. Say you got hit by lightning in your car —wouldn't hurt you because the car itself is a Faraday cage."

"Okay, I get that, Bill Nye, but what does it have to do with me, and our project?"

Pilot looked pleased with himself. "I'm glad you asked, Miss Sassy." He pulled out a sheet of paper on which he'd drawn something that resembled a birdcage. Inside of it, he'd drawn a figure, a ballerina, Boh, capturing her perfectly in mid-flight, her long limbs angled and graceful, mirroring the lightning bolts that were hitting the cage.

"Wow."

"You like it? The idea?"

"I like the idea and the sketch. How the hell did you catch my likeness so well?"

Pilot grinned. "It's a useful skill to have. But, seriously, what do you think? A series of movement and power. I'm not saying we do the entire shoot in a Faraday cage; I see it as a progression, maybe you in the cage at first, even hiding from the element until later in the series when you're almost battling with it. I'm rambling."

"You are, a little, but I think it's a great start." She looked back at the sketch. She loved the visual of it. "Would you do it as a modern piece or retro? Because I'm think this would look great as sepia-toned thing ... God, listen to me. You're the photographer."

Pilot leaned forward. "Listen, this is a collaboration, Boh. We work together. Besides ... you can order me around any time you like."

"Ha, don't say that," she laughed, blushing. Pilot traced a line with his fingertip across her palm and smiled at her.

"Will you be late for class?"

She shook her head. "I'm not scheduled until nine. I'm glad you called."

"Are you free for dinner later?"

She made a face. "That I don't know. Kristof is still running Vlad and me ragged and his usual trick is to keep us late on weeknights. Yesterday, I was lucky. May I let you know later?"

"Of course. Look, I have meetings in Manhattan all day so any time you have free to talk about the project, I'd appreciate it, but I also know you have to have downtime, so I won't be offended if you cry off."

Boh secretly thought that she would love to spend her downtime with Pilot, but she also knew she had to be mature about this. The last thing she wanted him to think was that she was a star-struck schoolgirl with a crush. He was studying her as if trying to read her mind.

"This has all happened quickly, and Boh, I want you to know—" he faltered and looked away, "I kissed you."

"Yes."

"That wasn't very professional of me, and I'm aware you might think it's something I always do with my subjects. You can believe me or not, but I don't. I haven't. I've never been a player, despite what my ex-wife might say. If any of this makes you uncomfortable, I want you to tell me."

He was letting her down, obviously regretting kissing her. Boh swallowed the lump in her throat and nodded.

"I appreciate that." She could feel her cheeks burning. Here, in front of her, was a world-famous photographer, and when she'd searched him on the Internet, she'd been disbelieving that the man who had kissed her and joked around with her could be so very out of her league. "I do have to focus on the performance," she said quietly, but managed to smile at him, "as well as our project."

"I would never put your job in jeopardy, Boh, I promise." He smiled at her. "Boh ... I'm twice your age, divorced, and a wreck. You deserve more."

Boh wondered that the atmosphere between them had changed so suddenly from fun-loving to serious. "Pilot, I'm not someone who craves other people's company, in fact, I actively seek out situations where I can be alone. But I like spending time with you."

Pilot smiled. "Same here. Friends?"

"Friends."

PILOT WALKED Boh back to the ballet company and then bid her goodbye. As he walked back to the car, he shook his head. He'd stayed awake all night thinking about her and the usual doubts about his self-worth had come flooding in. He'd tried to argue that he shouldn't ignore the kind of chemistry that had been instantly there between them, but neither could he bring Boh into his shitty life at the moment. Once he was free of Eugenie, maybe.

So he'd given Boh an out.

Damn it.

His phone buzzed, and he saw it was his mother calling. "Hey, Mom."

"Hey, cutie. How are you? I haven't heard from you for a few days."

Pilot smiled to himself. Since his divorce, Blair Scamo had been more attentive than usual, worried that her son would fall into one of the depressive moods he was prone to. Blair had disliked Eugenie from the beginning, but she also respected her son's decisions and had been polite and kind to Eugenie throughout the marriage. She'd also seen Pilot at his most broken, when Eugenie's cruelty had taken his pride, his confidence, and on more than one occasion, his health.

"I'm ..." He was about to tell her that he was good, but he knew it would be a lie. Eugenie's latest visit had put a strain on him that he was finding hard to get past. He sighed. "Genie came to see me the other day. She wants a baby."

"Oh, for the love of God." He could hear his mother's anger. "I've said it before, Pilot. You need to ghost her, cut her out entirely."

He was silent for a moment, and when Blair spoke again, her tone was softer. "Sometimes I forget the man I raised. You're too good, Pilot, and I know that sounds strange. You were a victim of domestic abuse, Pilot—"

"Don't say that, Mom, please." Pilot winced at his mother's words.

"Don't be a macho man. There's no shame in admitting that, Pilot. It happens to the strongest people, the very strongest. The strong and the good. It's time, my boy."

THE TROUBLE WAS—PILOT was embarrassed. Humiliated on more than one occasion by Genie in public, physically and emotionally attacked in private. Subconsciously, he touched the half-moon scar at the corner of his right eye. A broken champagne bottle that time. It could have ended his career, and he had no doubt that was exactly what Genie had wanted—to hurt him in the worst way.

He knew what he had to do. A new apartment, try to keep the details out of the press. He should keep the one in his present building as a decoy. It was a start.

That was the other reason he had backed away from Boh. Eugenie's jealousy knew no limits and if she found out he was seeing someone else—someone so much younger and, in Pilot's opinion, far more beautiful and sweet—he couldn't bear the thought of Boh getting caught up in the ferocity of Genie's rage.

God, what a fucking mess of a life. He could feel the black cloud descending on him. He stopped and got his bearings. What was next? What was he on his way to do?

He checked his schedule on his phone and turned down Broadway, making his way to his studio.

Work. Work was what would push the pain away, although he wished with all his being that when he reached his studio, Boh would be there to hold him in her arms.

CHAPTER EIGHT

"Where the fuck have you been?"

Kristof's rage filled the studio, and, humiliated, Boh put her bag down before she answered him, trying to keep her voice steady. "I wasn't scheduled until nine, Kristof, and it's ten of now."

She saw Serena smirk. Kristof's dark eyes burrowed into hers. "So we're adding illiterate to tardy now?" He stormed outside of the studio and Boh saw him rip the class schedules from the corkboard on the wall outside the studio. Her heart sank. Clearly, there had been another late schedule change. Kristof came in and shoved the piece of paper at her. Sure enough, under her name was "Mendelev, Studio 6, 8 a.m."

"I didn't see this. When I left last night, it was still—"

"I don't want your fucking excuses, Boh. Get changed into the white leotard."

Ah. He often made them change into different clothes to better see the lines of their bodies when they danced. She grabbed her bag and headed out of the door.

"No. Get changed—here."

Boh stopped, shocked. A murmur went around the class.

What the hell? Kristof's eyes gleamed with malice. "Do it. Clearly, you don't mind stripping down for Pilot Scamo, so, so shy?"

"What the hell are you talking about?"

"You're fucking him. We all know about it. So, come on. Get changed and let us all see what he sees."

Serena gave a chuckle and Boh shot her a fierce glare. "Who I see in my private time is my business, but you're wrong. Pilot Scamo and I are just friends and I have no intention of stripping off just because you're in one of your petty tempers, Kristof."

Boh heard the gasp from some of her cohort, and she was shocked at her own response to the man. She saw anger ripple across his face. "Strip or get out," he said steadily. "And someone else will dance the lead in the workshop."

Bastard. She would not let him take what she had worked so hard for. Pulling her arms into her sweatshirt, she yanked the bottom of it down to cover her ass and stripped off her pants and underwear. Kristof watched her in amusement as she deftly changed into her leotard without exposing any intimate parts.

"There, that wasn't so hard, was it? Now, first positions."

Boh was still angry at the end of the class, and they all walked back to the changing rooms, she hooked her finger in the back of Serena's top and yanked her back. "Keep your filthy little rumors to yourself, bitch."

Serena extracted herself from Boh's grip and gave her the finger. "We're all pretty sick of this precious little virgin routine, Dali. No one believes it. So fuck you and your skeevy photographer."

Boh, incensed, lunged for the other girl, but Grace and Fernanda pulled her back. "Fuck off, Serena," Grace said, and, snickering, Serena walked away. "Ignore her, Boh, she's just being—"

"A little cu—"

"Boh! This isn't like you. Come on." Grace hauled her away, down to the cafeteria. When they were seated, Boh sighed and folded her arms on the table, resting her head on them.

"Sorry, Gracie," she said, "I'm a grouch today."

Gracie studied her. "You were already gone when I left the apartment this morning. Where did you go?"

Boh could feel her face burn. "I had a breakfast meeting with Pilot Scamo."

Grace smiled. "You like him."

"I do, but this is a working relationship." He'd made that clear, she thought sadly. She tried to smile at Grace. "But he's going to be working with all of us, and so I would hate for any rumors to get back to him, embarrass him. Untrue rumors."

"You're sweet, but I think Scamo can look after himself. He is a phenomenal photographer." Grace was flicking through some of Pilot's images on her phone. She smiled at her friend. "If anyone can capture you, Boh, it's him. I can't wait to see what he does."

"With all of us," Boh corrected but couldn't help the little smile that escaped from her. Grace laughed and squeezed her arm.

"You know what, Boh? If you have a crush, that's okay. You can date who you want. You should date, at your age. How come you never have?"

Boh felt the usual dread seep into her chest, the fear that always followed when someone questioned her solitary life. But before she could answer her, their attention was caught by the elderly woman walking slowly into the room, her gaze wheeling around, her expression one of confusion. Grace and Boh were up immediately to go to her side.

"Madam Vasquez? Are you okay?"

The elderly woman smiled at them both. "June, Sally, how lovely to see you."

Grace and Boh exchanged a glance. Eleonor Vasquez was a former prima ballerina, one of the world's greatest, with one of the longest careers of a dancer ever, her career mercifully unhampered by serious injury. What ended her career eventually was the scandal of her lifelong love affair with Celine Peletier becoming public in an age when homosexuality and lesbian relationship were still taboo.

Vasquez, a firebrand from Argentina, had made a public statement about her love for the Frenchwoman. "My dancing career was my passion," she told reporters, "but my love Celine is my life."

The two women had been together for over 50 years now, but time had caught up with Eleonor a decade ago. Dementia. The ballet company, loyal to her to the last, allowed her to live with Celine in one of the company's apartments next to the studios, and even allowed her to "teach" still. A few of the dancers would give the extra time to be taught by this living legend, Boh and Grace among them. They didn't mind being whoever she wanted them to be for that hour.

Serena and some of the others wouldn't give that time, dismissing the elderly woman as a "demented fool." But the love Eleonor and Celine shared was an inspiration to most of the troupe, and their support, Boh knew, meant the world to Celine Peletier.

She and Grace walked Eleonor back to her apartment now, where they were met by an exasperated looking Celine. "You wandered off again?"

Eleonor beamed at her lover. "How lovely to see you, Petal," she said, using her pet names for Celine. Celine rolled her eyes and steered Eleonor into the apartment. She smiled gratefully at Boh and Grace. "Thank you, girls. Now, my little white swan, let's get you to bed."

Grace closed the door quietly and the two women walked slowly back down to the studios.

"Puts any little annoyance into perspective, doesn't it?"

Boh nodded. "It does." She recalled the way Eleonor and Celine looked at each other and her heart ached. To have so much love and to risk losing your partner to the relentless horror of dementia ... she couldn't imagine. Their love made her crush on Pilot seem even more ridiculous. He was a grownup and she was just a kid ... no matter if their attraction had been so palpable it was insane.

"What's on your mind?" Grace asked her, but Boh just nodded.

"Nothing. Let's go dance."

SERENA SNORTED the ivory white line from the table and wiped her nostrils, grinning at Kristof as she laid back on top of him. "That was a particularly cruel trick you played on little Miss Perfect this morning, but I have to say, I enjoyed it."

She straddled his naked form and reached for his cock, stroking it, trying to get him hard again. He was smoking a joint, watching her carefully. She knew this look in his eyes; it was spite. His cock remained limp, and she gave up, rolling onto the side of his bed and getting up.

"Where are you going?"

"To pee."

She went into the bathroom and sat down on the toilet. Sex with Kristof had been thrilling at the start. The first day she had arrived at the company, already an established member of another rival company, he had singled her out, asked her to stay after the final class of the day.

He'd fucked her in his office, bending her over his desk and thrusting hard. Since then, two years ago, they'd continued to screw each other but Serena had been disappointed that it had gotten her no further than soloist. She'd begged Kristof to make her principal after the former lead had moved on, and she had thought she was close to it. But then Kristof had seen Boheme Dali dance and promoted her to principal instead.

He'd pacified a furious Serena with even more sex, and as many appetite-suppressing drugs and cocaine as she could handle, but still, it rankled. Serena knew Boh was the superior dancer—hell, Serena secretly loved to watch the other girl dance—but her upbringing meant she expected nothing to be denied to her. So she made Boh's life a misery.

And she knew something about Boheme that no one else did. Crashing a party at Boh and Grace's apartment, she'd seen a handwritten letter addressed to Boh and had pocketed it on a whim. She hadn't imagined the contents of that letter would be so salacious, so useful. Boh's daddy was a bad, bad man. Boh's pure virginal act was just that, an act, even if she was the victim of her pedophile father. Serena had kept Boh's secret, not out of charity, but she was waiting for the opportune moment to drop it on her.

Maybe that moment was coming sooner than later, Serena pondered now as she washed her hands. She toyed with telling Kristof about the letter but decided against it. Her erstwhile lover was already too damn preoccupied with Boh as it was. She looked in the mirror, seeing her strawberry blonde hair was messy and was sticking to the sweat on her forehead. She splashed water on her face and smoothed down her hair. As she walked back in the bed, Kristof was scribbling in his notebook, working out choreography, she knew.

She laid back beside him on the bed. "Finally decided on the playlist yet?"

Kristof nodded. "We're doing The Lesson whether Liz likes it or not. It's the perfect ballet for a sex and death theme. Darkness, obsession. For Chrissake, Nureyev danced it, so I don't understand Liz's reticence."

"I think she's worried about the violence against woman thing in these days of Me Too," Serena said dryly. She selected a ready rolled joint from Kristof's silver cigarette case and lit it, coughing immediately and grimacing. She'd never liked pot. It made her goofy, whereas the coke gave her superhuman energy. Kristof looked annoyed and snatched the joint from her.

"Don't waste it. This is top market shit."

Serena looked at him slyly. "Who are you getting clean pee from? I know you must be getting it from someone, one of the guys. Who owes you a favor like that, Kristof?"

His eyes glinted dangerously and Serena felt a frisson of fear shoot through her. That Kristof was mercurial was well-known but at that moment, Serena saw something else in his eyes and the word that shot into her brain was ... unhinged. Shit.

"Never mind." She reached for his cock again and this time, she did get him hard. She straddled him, gently taking his notebook from him and running her hands over his chest as she slowly impaled herself on his cock.

Kristof's expression changed from annoyance to satisfaction as they began to fuck again and as Serena moved on top of him, he grabbed her hair and fisted it in his hands, crushing his mouth against hers then groaning, "Oona ... Oona ... I'm sorry, I'm sorry ..."

Serena waited until after he had fallen asleep to cry.

If you want to continue reading this story, you can get your copy from your favorite vendor by searching for the title:

The Virgin's Dance
An Older Man/Younger Woman Romance

You can also find the e-book version by typing this link in your computer's browser:

https://www.hotandsteamyromance.com/products/the-virgin-s-dance-an-older-man-a-younger-woman-romance

OTHER BOOKS BY THIS AUTHOR

The Virgin's Baby: A Forced Marriage Romance (Son's of Sin #2)

Having a stranger's baby wasn't a thing I'd ever dreamt of doing...

https://www.hotandsteamyromance.com/collections/frontpage/products/the-virgin-s-baby-a-forced-marriage-romance-sons-of-sin-2

∿

The Mountain Man's Secret: An Older Man Younger Woman Romance

Lust. Lies. Double lives.

I came to the mountains after my old partners murdered my wife.

https://www.hotandsteamyromance.com/collections/frontpage/products/the-mountain-mans-secret-an-older-man-younger-woman-romance

∿

Her Dark Secret: A Billionaire & A Virgin Romance

(Attico) She is the last person I should fall in love with ...
And yet it was inevitable.

https://www.hotandsteamyromance.com/collections/frontpage/products/her-dark-secret-a-billionaire-a-virgin-romance

Boss' Secret Baby: A Billionaire's Second Chance Romance

He was supposed to be one of us. That's who I fell in love with, not the greedy bastard he became. How was I to know he was destined to be a part of my family…in more ways than one?

https://www.hotandsteamyromance.com/collections/frontpage/products/boss-secret-baby-a-billionaire-s-second-chance-romance

The Doctor's Promise: A Single Daddy Romance

I never thought I'd love again.

After I lost my fiancée, my entire focus has been on my son.

Except…

https://www.hotandsteamyromance.com/collections/frontpage/products/the-doctors-promise-a-single-daddy-romance

You can find all of my books here

Hot and Steamy Romance

https://www.hotandsteamyromance.com

ABOUT THE AUTHOR

Mrs. Love writes about smart, sexy women and the hot alpha billionaires who love them. She has found her own happily ever after with her dream husband and adorable 6 and 2 year old kids.

Currently, Michelle is hard at work on the next book in the series, and trying to stay off the Internet.

"Thank you for supporting an indie author. Anything you can do, whether it be writing a review, or even simply telling a fellow reader that you enjoyed this. Thanks

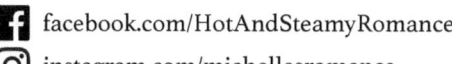

facebook.com/HotAndSteamyRomance
instagram.com/michellesromance

COPYRIGHT

©Copyright 2020 by Michelle Love - All rights Reserved

In no way is it legal to reproduce, duplicate, or transmit any part of this document in either electronic means or in printed format. Recording of this publication is strictly prohibited and any storage of this document is not allowed unless with written permission from the publisher. All rights are reserved. Respective authors own all copyrights not held by the publisher.

www.ingramcontent.com/pod-product-compliance
Lightning Source LLC
LaVergne TN
LVHW021704060526
838200LV00050B/2504